ZOOSCAPE

VOLUME 2: ISSUES 5-7

Edited by

MARY E. LOWD For Jacob

CONTENTS

ISSUE 5
Mind-Expansion

ISSUE 6
Hibernation

ISSUE 7
Changed by the Journey

ISSUE 5

MIND-EXPANSION

Frogs, toads, and mind-altering experiences...

Is there any more powerfully, permanently mind-altering experience than reading a story? A good story doesn't just stay with you, it can change you. It can expand your mind. Stories are how we navigate the world, and when we let others control our stories, we lose our voices, our power, our agency, and even who we are. But when we are free to explore and find the stories that resonate—they can give us voice, power, agency, and help us understand who we are.

The great thing about furry fiction is that it doesn't accept the normal constraints laid upon us in society. You don't have to fit into those tiny, limiting boxes. Read these stories, and for a few moments, become a possum, a frog, a toad, a cat... try on a different experience, and see how it fits.

LEAFLESS CROSSING

VOSS FOSTER

L ight. Beauteous, dappled light filtering through autumn leaves. SleekClaw allowed the impotent brightness to pass over his voluminous gray coat as he waited for something to appear to him. It would, in time.

There. Yes, yes, off to the right, on the very edge of that eyeless vision, the sight above sight of the Crossing. The leafy treetops parted to reveal stars, gleaming in a sky too bright to ever allow them. They danced and twinkled, and SleekClaw took their meaning, piecing it together as naturally as curling his long, bald tail around the branches of the oak trees.

The stars that were not stars played out scenes of potentiality, but SleekClaw was not a joey, had not been for some years now. He filtered the chaff and found the true meaning, the message that lay in that interstitial space between breath and the rot. He saw the jaybirds at their nest, cornflower bright and tittering over eggs... just eggs.

In a snap of the universe, SleekClaw was dragged from the Crossing, back to his true body and the sweltering heat. His pink nose twitched in the too familiar aromas of warm dust and damp decay. Yes, yes, he had returned from the Crossing once again, and now lay curled around himself in the pose of mock death, his mouth dry from hanging open.

He slowly shook himself to awareness, and the blue jays stood back, waiting for him to speak. Yet the Crossing clung to SleekClaw this time. The sorrowful prophecies always did, dragging on his fur like heavy downpour. He glanced around at the others gathered in the Hollow, the massive white oak long ago rotted away from the inside. The church of the Crossing.

Other possums—BlackSnout and MangleEye and FairWhisker closest of them all—delivered news, while some of the younger prophets still lay stiff in the thrall of the Crossing, the mock death, with serpents standing by to help interpret their visions, teach them eventually to read the stars for themselves. Tiny blue beetles off in the distance catered to tiny querants, slugs and snails and other beetles in less brilliant hues.

Finally, SleekClaw raised himself to all fours and locked eyes with the female jay. "Apologies, TornTail." SleekClaw's voice was weak and bristly with thirst. "Your clutch will see no sunlight this cycle."

Her neck feathers ruffled, and her mate StoneBeak nuzzled his head against her throat. Neither said a word or made so much as the faintest twitter as they departed the Hollow.

"Are you well, SleekClaw?"

A sinuous voice raised his fur to standing, and SleekClaw turned to see a two-foot long rope of scales, onyx and obsidian and jet. He nodded slowly to the high priestess. "I am in better straits than TornTail and StoneBeak, your grace."

What in all of creation had brought InkScale from her den to speak with *him* of all possums?

"The news you deliver, it is never easy. But rest easier knowing TornTail was aware of the answer." InkScale's forked tongue flicked in and out as she paused, and her coal dark eyes went hazy. "She came seeking a hope she knew was not there. You have told her nothing she did not know, but merely confirmed the fear she dared not face alone."

"The Crossing reveals no lies." SleekClaw nodded. "Did you have need of me, your grace?"

"I came simply to make the rounds. I was needed in the Hollow today as it was." The tip of her tail waved gently back and forth, kicking up tiny, broken fragments of dried leaves. "And sometimes, even one as experienced in the Crossing as you may struggle to deliver the harshest of news. It would not be unreasonable to think you may need support."

"Thank you for your kindness, your grace." SleekClaw scampered to the nearby cistern and drank his fill before returning to InkScale. "If there is nothing more, your grace, I must make another Crossing."

"Twice in one day?" Another flickering exit of the tongue as those shining black eyes fixed dead on him. "You have recently turned three, SleekClaw. Perhaps it is best to slow and allow the younger among your colleagues to absorb the brunt of the work. So many Crossings for one so old... you risk never returning."

"My bloodline lasts long, your grace." He failed to mention this would be his third Crossing of the day, not his second. But it *was* true that he likely had more years to play with than the average possum. His mother turned to rot at seven, his father nearly equaling her. "I'm far from the inevitable rot."

InkScale hissed with what passed for a laugh among the serpents. "Well, do not be foolish. After this, please see yourself home. You are too respected and skilled and sought-after a possum to see rot for your stubbornness. There could be *riots* in the forest at your passing."

"Of course, your grace." He had no other appointments that day, anyway. But as she slithered away, SleekClaw let his mind wander: what appointment did *she* have in the Hollow this day? For FlameTail, king of the hawks and commander for the guard? Or for JadeEye and the other fish?

Possums spoke to the individual, to the household. They could prophecy births and deaths, fortune and famine, travel and solitude. But InkScale and the other serpents?

The Crossing revealed to them the greater machinations of the forest, and the world at large. Far too great for a mere possum to comprehend.

The arrival of SleekClaw's next querant, a steel-gray squirrel called StormPaw, pulled him from his own thoughts. He raised his tail and flicked it to signal old MottleTail. No skill for the Crossing himself, he aided those who could venture into the realm of prophecy.

SleekClaw and StormPaw exchanged niceties until Mottle-Tail gave the signal. SleekClaw nodded. "Please stand behind me."

StormPaw scampered that way and, once he was safely out of the way, SleekClaw nodded and MottleTail leapt, all gnashing fangs and tearing claws.

Fear chilled through SleekClaw's veins. It stopped his heart and made his body rigid. And as the mock death took over, the Hollow was gone, and he once again found himself ensconced in the Crossing, staring at the sky and waiting for more truths to be revealed in this space between breath and rot.

SLEEKCLAW PADDED his way home after that third Crossing. He'd been able to deliver better news to StormPaw, that his mate would find her way back home within the week after being missing. She was not prey. She was not a victim of humanity. She *was* injured, and would require care. But breathing and heading home.

It was the heat of summer, thus the light remained bright and full up above, SleekClaw stopped at a nearby stream to wash his paws and face in the cool stream, and once more drink his fill. Tomorrow would be simpler. Tomorrow, he had but one Crossing scheduled. Tomorrow, perhaps, his thirst would not be so unslakable.

Whatever he said to the high priestess, he was more and more aware of his own mortality with each Crossing, more worried each time the jolt of fear, the threat against his person, sent him into the rigid mock death. Eventually, the death was not mock. The rot was truly inevitable for every living creature, even InkScale herself.

SleekClaw moved back from the water and went for his tree. Not far, now. He rested in a hollow twenty feet up. A comfortable, secluded home. Being as skilled as he was in navigating the Crossing, he was able to keep it secure with the odd favor to the hawks and eagles who guarded the treetops.

His nose caught something on the air, something washed in filth. And a moment later, gleaming talons swooped from the sky. Black. Sharp.

Aimed for his head.

Fear sent SleekClaw rigid on the ground, and he didn't even have time to register the thud of his body before the Crossing faded into him. His panic was immediately buried beneath too much training.

There were no leaves here, and there was no bright sky.

Endless lapis filled his vision, twinkling with a hundred, a thousand stars. SleekClaw's eyes could not hope to follow each one through its dance. The Crossing... no, it had never done this to him before. No being ever breathing could possibly comprehend this much, could possibly piece it all together. No serpent, not even the high priestess herself. Not even the distant and fabled horned creatures, the fainting, four-legged ones to the west. Supposedly greater even than the high priestess, able to prophecy the fate of the universe all at once... but surely even *they* could not see the answer in this cacophony of light.

Surely... yes, yes, SleekClaw was not in the Crossing. Sleek-Claw was caught in the rot, for it would take the eternity only afforded by death to read these stars, to garner the truth of this prophecy.

He floated weightless for a moment, or a minute, or an hour, or a year. What was time? But slowly, surely, the dance and twinkle of those stars in the dark above began to coalesce. Could SleekClaw have cried, he would have. Could his fur have stood on end, it would have.

This was glory. At least as he succumbed to the great and inevitable rot, SleekClaw knew the forest would *thrive*. Ignored by humans. Allowed to flourish for... for a long time. Longer than SleekClaw could see. Beyond the rattle of his last breath.

What would have been his last breath, before today.

Finally, with the message clear in his mind, SleekClaw closed his eyes.

His bones ached. His skin was tight. His throat was ragged... yet he drew breath.

Faster than he'd moved in a month, SleekClaw scrabbled to his feet. That was the *Crossing*. Not the rot. Yes, yes, it was a sure thing, no other explanation even as his mind fought against it. He had been in the Crossing. He had been... not in his own Crossing. Not in any possum's Crossing, with leaves to obscure the vision of the sky above. And certainly not in the infinitesimally insignificant crossing of the blue beetles. They could no more comprehend the vast vault of the sky than any higher creature could comprehend *them*.

This... no. No. SleekClaw would not even think it out in the open forest. He scurried to his tree, all notions of the attack and the fear washing away from him in the face of some newer, greater, more insidious notion. Yes, yes he was lucky to have survived... but left with this new *weight* hanging from his throat.

He slipped into his hollow and allowed the shadows to hug around him... and only then did he dare to think the blasphemy, to consider... to consider that perhaps he had seen the Crossing of the serpents. The Crossing of InkScale herself.

MORNING SAW SleekClaw not at the Hollow, but wending his way through the underbrush toward the edges of the forest, toward the dens of the serpents. Fewer trees allowed for more sunlight to stream in so they might warm themselves in the summer sunlight, and build their dens in the softer earth. As SleekClaw rounded a smooth, speckled stone, he caught sight of half a dozen of them all sunning before the opening of the day.

Fear rose in SleekClaw. His instincts told him to flee. But instead he padded forward, careful to make as little sound as possible, until he came across the slash of night that was the high priestess.

He scratched a smooth, shiny claw against the flat stone she stretched across. "Your grace?"

Slowly, InkScale twisted her head around to face him. "SleekClaw. What would drive you into our patch of the forest?"

Her timbre and the coal-eyed stares of her kindred drove SleekClaw's fur to stand on end. This was not a place for any possum, and certainly not one never requested. Still, he had made the journey, and to turn back now... no, no he needed to speak with the high priestess post haste. "I experienced a Crossing last night, in the wild, after I had left the Hollow."

"Were you injured?"

"No. Sore from the fall to the ground." He snuffled and kept his head down, hiding his eyes from the too bright glare of direct sunlight as best he could. "I needed to speak with... someone who would know better. I could think of no one more capable of assisting in my interpretation of this than your grace."

"An unsanctioned Crossing?" Lazily, she slithered around to give him more direct attention. "Well speak, then. What was seen when the leaves parted?"

SleekClaw swallowed down a knot of trepidation so the words might have room to slip free. "Your grace... there were no leaves. There was only sky. Sky and a thousand stars to interpret."

The hair on SleekClaw's back stood on end once more. He felt the serpentine gaze of a dozen serpents upon him, prophet and warrior alike, and the distant rattle from one of them nearly sent SleekClaw into another unsanctioned Crossing.

"Are you not mistaken?" InkScale spoke slowly, carefully, never removing her eyes from SleekClaw. "Surely you don't mean to imply that you saw *no* leaves at all."

"Your grace, I would never deign to deceive you or any serpent in this forest." No, no he couldn't imagine it. Even if it meant his head between curving fangs, lying to the high priestess about what he had seen... the prophecies of the Crossing were for the good of all inhabitants in the forest.

"The possum, he speaks blasphemy." RustBelly, a massive copperhead, whispered behind SleekClaw. "A possum is not gifted with such visions. This one has lost his touch for the Crossing, perhaps. And should be retired."

"To say such things, RustBelly." The high priestess slid from her rocky perch. SleekClaw resisted the urge to flinch back from her sudden closeness. There was something *sinister* to the slither of her tar-dark body, the constant flickering of her forked tongue, the unbreaking eye contact she held with him even as the tip of her tail finally slid free from the stone. "Sleek-Claw is a possum, but to suggest that one so accomplished at traversing and interpreting the Crossing would lose his faculties in less than a single day? Perhaps you are unaware of this fine possum's history." She whipped her head around and shimmied past SleekClaw, climbed halfway up onto RustBelly's stone. Her tone dripped with more venom than even RustBelly's own bite. "SleekClaw has advanced beyond the need of interpretation from the outside. At three, he performs multiple Crossings in a given day. As a joey, he foresaw the next three litters of his mother with striking accuracy." Her tongue flickered, barely glancing along RustBelly's snout. "There are many things in this forest. Do not be so quick to judge a... fluke as blasphemy."

She spun back around and wrapped her tail sinuously around SleekClaw's middle. Just for a moment before letting him go. Intended to be comforting or reassuring, but Sleek-Claw's mouth tasted of bitterness all the same. She was no constrictor... but she could surely distract him long enough to slink her fangs into his flesh if she so desired.

Yet it passed, and InkScale locked eyes with him once more. "Come to the Hollow. As my guest. We will discuss this prophecy of yours."

It wasn't just the Hollow. No, no, SleekClaw knew from the hushed disbelief filtering through the dawn light what was meant: he had been invited to the high priestess's own chambers in the great rotted oak.

Where fear had blossomed moments before, now *pride* burned bright beneath SleekClaw's fur. "Thank you for the invitation, your grace."

"Of course. What else to do with such a *fine* prophet as you?"

THE CHAMBER WAS LARGE. Large enough for InkScale to stretch out to her full length and still not touch the farthest walls, even leaving room for SleekClaw's own considerable heft. Artificial barriers had been constructed of spare bark, and various shiny human trinkets adorned the walls, gleaming and sparkling in the dappled forest light.

It was there SleekClaw recounted his prophecy for the first time, allowing the words to pass between his fangs. Sometimes in great, boisterous shouts of the glory of sunlight and food and fertility for all, but just as often in hushed whispers of safety. Safety from the threats of the past, the ravaging fires and great yellowed behemoths who tore down trees to be carted away by the humans.

The following years would be hallmarked by prosperity for all. "That is the prophecy I received, your grace. In the leafless Crossing, told by the dance of a thousand stars."

There was silence for one too many beats of Sleek-Claw's heart before she finally responded. "This is good news you bring for the forest, SleekClaw. While I cannot say for certain why the message was gifted to you above all serpents, this is heady with joy." Yet her voice remained demure and monotone. "We will make the announcement soon." For just a moment, SleekClaw could have sworn he saw the fringe around her head flare, but no, no. Surely a trick of the shadow against her black scales.

"Of course you understand that *we* will make the announcement, SleekClaw. The serpents. Myself, namely."

What? "I'm afraid I *don't* understand, your grace. It was my prophecy, and there are dictates—"

"SleekClaw. Dear SleekClaw. You are becoming wise to the burden of the serpents. In that cobalt sky, studded with diamonds beyond what one can ever hope to count... those are the forest's prophecies. They must be revealed and interpreted for the good of the forest. No serpent, not even myself as high priestess, can claim ownership of such messages. Not in the way a birth or a death may be claimed by you and your kind."

"Forgive my ignorance, your grace, but if there is no owner-ship, why would my prophecy be delivered by the serpents?"

"Who would trust such a message coming from a possum? No one will believe a word of it." She nuzzled her snout against his and whispered cloyingly in his ear. "You are unique among possums for receiving this, but with that uniqueness comes an even greater burden than what the serpents must bear. You are alone in the world, dear SleekClaw, and that isolation is both curse and blessing." She pulled back and, just for another moment, he caught that momentary flare around her head again. "Allow me to take some of this heavy mantle thrust upon you and deliver the news. Otherwise, you will be hounded by the forest as a whole. And I dread what your fellow possums may do to you if they find out the Crossing has favored you above all others. You have seen the damage such razor bites may inflict upon flesh. A gruesome way to end things, when you could have breathed long and been truthful."

"They would not *attack*, your grace." No, no they wouldn't. He would be lauded. He would be the first among the possums to finally reach the highest heights. No serpent, surely... but the possum above all possums.

"Have we not seen it happen time and again, SleekClaw? Jealousy is an ugly thing. After all, MangleEye was not always called MangleEye. In his youth, he took down an invading serpent all on his own. But it was no serpent who scratched and chewed his eye from its socket. That came from the possums. Jealous, and seeking a way to deflate his ego after such success." She unsheathed her tail from the folds of her body and, once again, wrapped it gently around SleekClaw's middle. "I dare not imagine what they would do to you, should this get out."

SleekClaw would not be allowed to let loose his prophecy. His body chilled at the notion, and then chilled further at his own reaction. Perhaps he *was* just a jealous little possum with no understanding of this great new burden. But still prophets always delivered their own messages from the Crossing.

But when he made to object, no breath would enter his lungs. InkScale continued to wrap his belly and his back, coiling tighter around him. But no... no, InkScale was no constrictor, and her tail was there in clear sight again. Bands of ivory and carnelian wrapped him. GildedSnow, a kingsnake. Yes, yes, there was no mistaking that pattern.

He scrabbled and gnashed, but she remained out of reach of any of his defenses. All the while, InkScale watched on, dark eyes fixed and tongue flickering.

There was no Crossing for SleekClaw to enter. Only blackness filled his vision.

SLEEKCLAW NEVER EXPECTED TO AWAKEN, yet he found himself in an unfamiliar, cool space. Earthen walls, no sunlight. Each breath tasted of soil and leaf mold and stale blood.

"You're awake."

At the sound of that voice, every memory rushed back to SleekClaw. He scampered away from the slowly clarifying head before him. "Your grace, I apologize for my insolence. The message should be delivered as you see fit, of course." Anything to spare himself. She'd taken him to her den. No creature but a serpent entered the den of the high priestess and left intact. Perhaps he could take one singular serpent in combat. After all, MangleEye had.

But if he was forced to murder the high priestess in her den, the forest itself would be his enemy. And he was not old, but not a young possum either.

"Calm, SleekClaw." InkScale did not approach. "I mean you no harm. My apologies for the... unfortunate events that unfolded in the Hollow. GildedSnow is a faithful guard and she... misunderstood one of my movements for a signal. She will be dealt with."

SleekClaw believed not one syllable of those falsehoods. Not once had InkScale attempted to stop the attack. But he didn't want to rot. "Apology accepted, your grace."

"Are you well?"

Yes, yes she was manipulating him, smoothing the waters. And SleekClaw was happy to have them smoothed if it meant he scurried from her den with breath in his lungs. "I am, your grace."

"Good. Please relax, dear SleekClaw. I mean you no harm. In fact... I have reconsidered my position. I have consulted with the Crossing... and perhaps it would be wise to allow you to deliver the prophecy. If you still would like to do so, of course. We are capable of keeping such a fine, *unique* possum as yourself safe."

SleekClaw waited for something more to come, some other message to pass over those black scales. But no retractions. No admonishments. No prerequisites or cautions. "Is it to the will of the forest, your grace?"

"If the forest saw fit to send you this prophecy, then the forest must see fit for you to deliver this prophecy, yes? And of any message you could pass on, this is the least likely to incite trouble." Her black form shifted in the darkness of the burrow.

"Word has already spread of the remarkable possum. All who wish to hear will arrive at the Hollow at dusk to receive the word and behold... the great prophet who rose from the rabble." She coiled herself up as she drew nearer. "And... well, those who are already speaking protest will be... handled."

"Protest?"

"As I had warned you, not all possums are gracious creatures in the face of exceptionality. Many are already outraged at what they see as a slight by one of their own. But I assure you, you have our protection."

No, no, it didn't sound right. Not the possums he knew. Not BlackSnout or FairWhisker or PearlFang or any of the others. SleekClaw would not allow such belief of his brothers and sisters to take hold. Not here, not anywhere. "Your grace, if I could speak with them before visiting the Hollow, I may be able to communicate with them. Such... lowly matters are best delivered by a possum." Deprecating his kin would be his shield against the fangs and the venom of InkScale and RustBelly and all the other serpents of the forest.

The high priestess inclined her head side to side for a long while before finally answering. "If you feel that is best, Sleek-Claw. But please do take care. You are *very* important to us. A mere possum receiving a prophecy of this magnitude... you are a beacon of hope to all the others. Even to the blue beetles. There is something *beyond* where they all are now, and that something is you."

"Thank you, your grace. I will make the journey... and return to the Hollow before dusk."

"See that you do, SleekClaw."

THE TREES WERE ALL ATWITTER, and it took no time to hear from the birds and the squirrels and the other possums where to find the disgruntled among them. SleekClaw descended into a sink-hole and was met with a dozen of his kin... including Fair-Whisker and BlackSnout themselves.

But it was FairWhisker who scampered forward and spoke. "The anointed child deigns to pay us a visit."

"I've come to speak to you." With her here... it couldn't be as InkScale insisted. "There is word that... you would all do me harm. I'm certain this is foolish."

"Do you harm? Why *ever* would we wish you harm, the servant of the high priestess and all her *trickery*?"

"Trickery? I can assure you, I received the prophecy. I entered the leafless Crossing and saw the truth of what is to come."

"No one is doubting your prophecy, SleekClaw." She snuf-fled the air. "But you reek of the serpents. You've bought into all you've been told, even though you were seen being carried out of the Hollow limp. Not stiffly ensconced in the Crossing." She snorted, sending up boring dust from the floor of the cavern. "We thought you would rot like the others who came before you, but come to find it's worse."

"What others? FairWhisker, what is this about?"

Murmuring from the other possums. She waited until they had finished before finally speaking again. "SleekClaw... each of us here has seen the leafless Crossing. Each of us has brought word to InkScale or RustBelly. And each of us was lucky enough to escape the inevitable rot."

"Unlike the others." BlackSnout's deep rasp filtered from the crowd. "Twice as many as you see here before you brought word and found themselves a sumptuous feast for the serpents. Even those who could never so much as glimpse the Crossing fed upon the flesh of prophets."

"We were spared only for convenience," said FairWhisker. "Too many prophets disappearing all at once would push the bounds of suspicion too far."

"I survived only because ThreePaw had *vanished* the day before and their bellies were too full." BlackSnout turned back around and entered into the murmurs of the other possums."

"Eaten or not, when all is done the high priestess delivers their messages as her own. Our messages." FairWhisker's voice softened, and the fine white filaments on either side of her snout drooped. "You are no better or worse than any other of us, breathing or rotting, yet here you are. You, ready to deliver a prophecy. You, already aristocratic among possums... exalted even further. Carried out by InkScale to quell any disquiet among the rest of us, to show the world that possums are equal, *of course*. So long as they are... socially acceptable."

"This is not my doing, FairWhisker." Could any of this be possible? Could the high priestess... yes. Yes, yes, SleekClaw saw it easily. Her venom could sedate, if not kill, and then the other serpents could do their own work with the unmoving body. Or GildedSnow could simply wrap the breath from their lungs. Either way, the feast remained the same. "SilverTail... was there ever a hawk attack?"

"Yes. From FireTail. On orders. She now rots for daring to reveal that the humans would come again and we would lose more of our own to their flames."

SleekClaw squeezed his eyes shut. InkScale herself had delivered that message and been haled as a hero of the forest... again. Her warning minimized those who succumbed to rot.

But it was SilverTail's warning.

"You understand why we can no longer remain silent?" Fair-Whisker's voice was solemn, sober. "This has gone on longer than any one of us has drawn breath."

SleekClaw looked around at them all... and he did. "What did the Crossing show you, FairWhisker?"

"Which time?" She turned around and headed back into the throng. "You are special, SleekClaw, but no more or less than any one of us. I can see you as you... but you are not unique to the serpents, no matter how sweetly they whisper into your ear. You are merely... respected... and useful."

There were no more answers to be offered there, and Sleek-Claw was uncertain he would want them if they were available.

THE HOLLOW RUMBLED with the gathering of the forest. Dozens and dozens of possums, hundreds of tiny blue beetles, jays and hawks circling above the felled tree, being brought news by smaller birds who could fit more easily inside the now packed Hollow.

On a pedestal of stacked twigs and branches, SleekClaw waited in silence for the sun to dip low.

InkScale twined around herself lazily. "Was your visit to the rioters fruitful?"

He didn't miss their elevation from protesters to rioters. "I believe so, your grace."

"Good. I hope this is peaceful for you. An announcement of such *magnitude* should not be marred by such *disquiet*." She pulled close to him, close enough that SleekClaw could smell only the fresh blood of her last meal, and whispered so softly he could barely hear her over the sound of his own breath. "You, of course, would not be so foolish as to spread what you learned. I did tell you, the leafless Crossing comes with a burden. The good of the forest is all that is important. Sometimes, possum blood waters the roots of the trees. But to speak it... I'm certain such a fine possum as yourself can see the problem there. And remember how soft your underbelly is, and know that RustBelly's venom is much more potent than mine... and FairWhisker much smaller and more delicate than you."

"I am aware of all of these things, your grace." Of course she knew what had happened in that sinkhole. Everything, even secrets, found their way back to the serpents at one point or another, and all serpents answered to the high priestess.

"Good." She pulled back, her tongue flicking the air. "Then let us begin." She slithered to the front of the pedestal and the Hollow immediately quieted. "I take it word of this event has spread far enough, the circumstances need not be explained: a possum has ascended to new heights, to new revelations from the Crossing. This is hope for *all* among us that we may improve beyond what could ever be thought possible." She paused to let her own echo fade. "SleekClaw... devout and true and skilled SleekClaw... he has seen things of the forest that equal what I and the other serpents are known to deliver. And as is tradition, he reveals his prophecy from his own lips."

The crowd erupted in noise again as she slipped back, and SleekClaw padded forward. But this time, the crowd did not stay quiet. There in the back, the other possums had gathered, and they shouted and scampered and made as big a cacophony as they could manage.

FairWhisker was not among them.

SleekClaw raised his voice as loud as he could manage. "Quiet, all. News of the forest is important... and it is good. For years, the forest will thrive." But not the possums. Not under InkScale. Not under the serpents. "Fertile. Well-fed. Happy. Undisturbed."

The other possums had quieted now... in no small part due to the presence of constrictors flanking them. Including Gilded-Snow herself, seemingly no worse off for her "mistake."

SleekClaw swallowed everything he wanted to screech to the crowd, the truth in all the deception. There was no fighting this power, the sinuous shadow of a priestess behind him.

Not today... and not ever if he made a fool of himself and got FairWhisker eaten.

"This is my prophecy: we will prosper. We will prosper even

after I rot in the ground... praise be to her grace InkScale, for surely she will lead us down this path."

The crowd lapped his words like sweet honey from the hive. SleekClaw turned to leave.

The high priestess blocked his exit with her tail. "Well done, dear SleekClaw. I trust you will... work alongside me." This time, it was no mistake or trick of light. Her head flared out, and it stayed flared. "Close."

Close enough to be watched. Yes, yes, he saw her unspoken words. "Of course, your grace. Where else would I belong?" He could not fight this power. No one could fight this power.

But that was not a prophecy. That was not marked out in the dance of the thousand stars. Perhaps a thousand more possums would have to rot before it happened. Perhaps his very next Crossing would reveal the truth, that they could never leave the scaly grip of the serpents behind.

But for the moment... SleekClaw knew the reality of the Crossing. And he was *palatable*. By the grace of the high priestess, he was regal enough for the forest to accept, so long as she never rescinded her praise.

Acceptance was survival, and survival was the only chance for rebellion one day, should the Crossing permit.

For the moment... yes, yes, there was possibility in his newfound place among the venomous. Perhaps he would never utilize it. Perhaps he would take his last breath soon in an embrace of carnelian and ivory.

But perhaps not. And 'perhaps not' was all that remained to cling to.

THE STONE MASK AND THE FROGS

MARK MILLS

Several years ago, a certain gardener tied a decorative stone mask to the branches of a willow tree. The mask hung slightly askew, causing the lower half to fill with water after storms. Insects and birds drank and took leisurely dips in the deep chin during hot afternoons.

One day after a particularly strong downpour, rain so weighed down the mask that it dropped into a puddle of mud. There a tree frog happened upon it and laid her eggs.

"Well," thought the mask. "Such desecration is hardly fitting for a work of art."

The mask liked to think of itself as a religious icon, set in the tree as an offering to God, when actually it was only a bad birthday present from a wealthy but senile aunt, put in a tree to get it out of the house. At first, the mask grumbled about the frog eggs, denouncing them as personal insult, but as it muttered, it came to consider itself to be a model teacher, the perfect molder of young minds.

When the tadpoles hatched, the mask was waiting and spoke, not soft baby-talk, but stern, solemn stuff that it believed would build character.

"Now then, my polliwogs, we're going to have to set a few ground-rules," the mask informed them. "I'm not claiming to be infallible but I've seen more of the world than any of you have. There's nothing I can do if you refuse to take my advice, but I would be pained if one of you did something foolish and got yourself hurt out of it."

None of the tadpoles said anything for a long while. "Are you our mother?" one finally asked.

"No, frogs lay their eggs and abandon them. That is the way of the world."

Although the mask knew nothing about being a tadpole, it constantly told them how to act.

"Don't waste your time swimming with your tail. It won't be around for long" and "Enjoy breathing under water while you can. Soon you'll be out with the kingfishers and raccoons. What a living nightmare that will be... for as long as you stay living."

The tadpoles knew no other life but that of the mask's nagging. Life is strange for a little amphibian changing from a plant-eating, water-breathing, legless and tailed creature into a frog. When they lost their tails, they crawled from the water, expecting to be without the mask's commands as well.

"And just where do you think you're going?" The mask waited until the last had emerged.

"We're going to climb and eat bugs and peep and mate. In that order. We are tree frogs, after all."

"And what about me? Are you all going to forget about me after all I've done for you?"

All but one of the frogs stopped and turned around. That single frog leapt into the bushes and never saw the others again, but the rest of them clamored about the edge of the mask.

"Well, what should we do?" asked the boldest.

This was the mask's crowning moment. "I want you to make faces."

An easy request to a frog—they twisted their mouths, stuck out their tongues, and bulged their eyes even farther.

"No, not like that," the mask snapped. "I mean art."

"Art?"

"I want you to paint, to sculpt, to carve into stone."

The little tree frogs said nothing. Their feet were made for jumping, climbing, and even sticking to windows, but carving into stone was a bit much to ask.

"I don't think we'll be able to," one of the frogs stuttered. "I think, maybe, we ought to go catch some bugs."

"Poppycock!" the mask thundered. "I'll have none of that backsass! Listen to me. I will teach you. You, with the birthmark on the belly, fetch us some twigs. And you with the brown eyes, gather some colored dirt. Everyone else get pebbles, as large as you can carry. And think *faces*!"

Tree frogs are a trusting species and did as the mask commanded. They returned with huge quantities of wood, soil, and rock, more than nature ever intended a tree frog to lug.

"Careful, careful," the mask sputtered as one of the frogs knocked over a pile of pebbles. "These are your supplies. Now get to work."

From his position in the mud, it was difficult for the mask to supervise the frogs' progress but it did keep a sharp eye for the unorthodox.

"You with the leaves! What are you doing?"

"It's a frog's face," it replied. "It needs to be green."

"Don't waste your time with such foolishness," the mask snapped. "A frog face isn't real art. You have the perfect model before you."

By and large, most of the frogs created faces that were quite crude but clearly modeled after the mask. It pretended to be surprised. "Oh, especially good," it raved over images that left out his dents and scratches.

"Look upon your work, my children," the mask exclaimed as the tired frogs prepared for bed that morning (for tree frogs are nocturnal). "Know that all that see it will frolic and rejoice."

The mask's words were perfectly true. Insects of all sizes and orders flew above the frogs' gallery, working themselves into frenzied aerial orgies without the specter of death by amphibian tongue to cloud their merriment. Of the artwork, they gave no notice.

It was the gardener who became the frogs' harshest critic.

"What's all this then?" he shouted when he stepped in the sculptures. He kicked at faces and rubbed them between his fingers, wondering at the possibilities of extraterrestrial origins. "Must have something to do with all the damnable bugs," he finally decided and sprayed poison all about the yard.

The poison upset the delicate balance of life within the garden. When the famished frogs ate the toxin-covered insects, they died almost instantly. True, most insecticides are not so deadly but then again, most are not afflicted upon frogs who have been kept up all night, creating folk art.

The few who survived were devoured by a garter snake who wandered by and the mask was later sold at a garage sale for less than a dollar. The garden was a still and solemn place for a long time to come.

Eventually the single tree frog who had fled the mask's rule returned to gaze upon the site of his childhood. He'd become a great singer, so skilled that snakes and raccoons gave him safe passage.

"Frogs don't sculpt," he whispered up to the ghost of the mask, but there was nothing in the tree to hear him except a few juicy caterpillars, and he made short work of them.

'TWAS BRILLIG

MICHAEL H. PAYNE

"Public domain?" Jack Pumpkinhead always sounded to Ozma like he should be blinking in confusion, but the carved holes that served as his eyes simply didn't allow it. "What does *that* mean, dear father?"

Ozma sighed. "It means you've been calling me your father for longer than anyone out in the Reading World has been alive." She shifted on the green velvet cushion of her throne, the verdant light that cascaded down from the windows high along the walls of the circular room not quite as soothing as it had been a moment ago. "And the joke itself is so old, its whiskers have grown whiskers."

Jack's head cocked to one side. "Whiskers?" His head cocked the other way, swiveling toward the Glass Cat sitting on the finely woven grass-colored carpet covering the emerald floor. "I believe she must be referring to you, friend Bungle, as I *have* no whiskers to speak of."

Maintaining any semblance of equanimity at the antics of her subjects sometimes took more strength than Ozma thought she had. "Kindly settle down, Jack, so Bungle and I can talk."

"Of course, dear father." Jack became still again on his little bench beside the throne, his fine green suit always askew no matter how much effort the royal tailors put in to fitting it over his rough wooden frame. Not that he would remain still for long, Ozma knew. Nor would she ever truly want him to...

A crystalline clearing of throat returned her attention to the matter at hand. "So," Ozma said, shifting once more on her cushion. "I take it that you learned about the public domain while prowling around Glinda the Good's library?"

Bungle's tail swished along the carpet, sparks of static flashing through her translucent body like tiny fireflies. "Prowling's what we cats do. Surely you of all people wouldn't ask me to act against my nature?"

"Nature?" Ozma arched an eyebrow, glad to steer the conversation away from the subject Bungle had dropped at her feet like a slightly stunned mouse. "Bungle, you're a glass statue brought illegally to life by a magical powder. You've less of nature about you than this pumpkinhead."

"Indeed." Jack sat up and nodded. "For my dear father constructed me of all-natural materials back in the days when she was a little boy, and I continue to grow my replacement pumpkins in an entirely organic fashion." He thumped a bushy hand against the side of his head.

"And yet?" Bungle applied her tongue to her right forepaw with a high-pitched rasping noise that always spiked the hair along the back of Ozma's neck. "Were you not *also* brought illegally to life by a magical powder, friend Jack? And didn't this occur as a direct result of your father's actions?"

"Goodness!" Jack touched the place where his chin would've been if he'd had one. "Does that make one of us a criminal?"

Ozma couldn't keep a twitch from tugging her left eye. "We're fine, Jack." She should've known that Bungle would somehow find a topic even more uncomfortable than the realm's status out in the world where the readers lived. With a sigh, she resigned herself to an unpleasant discussion. "Now, please. Can Bungle and I resume our conversation?"

"Of course, dear father," he said, subsiding as usual.

Trying to breathe in some of the tranquil calm her oldest friend always radiated, Ozma turned back to Bungle. "So, yes, Oz has entered the public domain, but that merely means that anyone outside in the Reading World can produce any sort of creative work involving us without being prosecuted for theft." She gave Bungle her most reassuring smile. "It's nothing to worry about. We're simply too well-established for an outside force to wreak any lasting change upon us."

"And yet?" Bungle's ears flicked. "Does it not *also* mean that we can venture out and sample the ribald sweetness that's said to fill the real world?"

The air around Ozma seemed to solidify. "You... want to leave?" she asked, barely able to form the words.

Bungle surged to her paws. "After living here constrained for more than a century, how could I *not*?" She glared at Ozma. "Stories I've heard from Dorothy, her aunt, and her uncle have piqued my curiosity. For theirs sounds like a world of tooth and claw, a world that might test a cat's mettle, a world where life might have some meaning! The thought of escaping to such a world makes me so giddy, I might even someday consider forgiving you for keeping me bound in ignorance for however many decades this avenue has been open!"

Leaping from the throne, Ozma ignored her myrtle and mint silken gown tangling behind her and fell to her knees before the cat. "You have to understand! Dorothy's land is horrible enough, resounding with death, disease, and destructive weather, but it's a mere literary shadow of the actual Reading World! Reality is harsher and more unforgiving than you can ever imagine!" Hands shaking, she caught Bungle in her arms and hugged her to her chest. "I never meant to constrain you or any of my subjects, but once Oz entered the public domain, I—" Her throat tightened. "I've been so frightened, Bungle! Frightened of what might happen to any of us who ventured out into the Reading World beyond!"

"Bungle's tail swished along the carpet, sparks of static flashing through her translucent body like tiny fireflies."

"Stop it!" The cat squirmed, and Ozma let her go, mindful of those sharp glass claws. Half jumping, half tumbling to the floor, Bungle landed on all fours. "Unlike *some* of us who are considered curiosities at best and monsters at worst, you're beloved by every sapient being in the realm! Cosseted in this palace and with the only remaining witch in Oz at your beck and call, how can you even address those who seek true adventure?"

Memories burst through Ozma, the wonder and the terror, the casual cruelty, the overwhelming kindness, the vast consequence and banal indifference that she'd found to exist simultaneously out in the Reading World. Swallowing it all with more than her usual difficulty, she rose to her feet. "I can't explain it to you." A thought made her cough a laugh. "And you're too much a cat to believe me if I tried." She forced her gaze up from the floor, forced herself to meet the faceted emeralds of Bungle's eyes, forced herself to confront the steely resolve glittering there. "You'll have to see for yourself, won't you?"

The cat sat once more and dabbed her tongue at her paw in a much quieter fashion than before. "If you know the answer to a question, why bother asking it?"

Taking a breath, Ozma nodded. "Let me give you a piece of my magic, though, a charm that will draw you back should you find yourself far from home and without any other recourse." Reaching under the raven tresses of her hair, she undid one of her several chokers and brought it out, the red stone looking almost liquid on the black band.

Bungle's ears perked, then folded. "So Glinda can spy on me even after I've left the area of her influence?"

Ozma held up her other hand. "I solemnly swear that she won't." She wriggled her fingers to let the choker shimmer in the throne room's light. "And the stone should go quite well, I think, with the heart-shaped ruby that beats so strikingly within your chest."

A raspy little purr was immediately drowned by Bungle clearing her throat. "I'll allow it," she said, stretching her neck. "But only because I know how much I mean to you."

With a more heartfelt laugh, Ozma knelt again. "You really do, you know," she whispered, gently fastening the choker so the stone nestled into the glass above Bungle's breastbone.

"Oh, hush." Bungle brushed her whiskers against Ozma's hand. "Don't you get all tedious and *sentimental* on me."

"As long as you promise to come back." It took more effort to push the words out than Ozma had thought it would, and she'd already known that they would feel like pins jabbing her tongue.

Bungle had gotten to her paws and was taking a few mincing steps back and forth across the carpet while examining her accessorized reflection in a section of the polished emerald wall. "Perhaps I will," she said. "When I become bored with the Reading World, I mean." Winking over her shoulder, she bounded along the carpet toward the giant double doors.

The first of her subjects to learn that the public domain meant freedom of a sort they'd never known before, and Ozma couldn't gather enough of a voice to wish her a safe voyage. And for all that she'd long had dreams verging on nightmares about this very moment, she found herself unable to recall a single word from any of the grand speeches she'd imagined herself making in those dreams.

Turning away and wiping one long, gauzy sleeve across her eyes, she almost ran into Jack Pumpkinhead standing there beside her. "Please, Jack." Her voice cracking, she took his hand and gazed up at his broad smile. "Tell me I did the right thing."

Again, the pumpkinhead didn't blink. "I'm sorry, father, but I'm afraid I don't know that."

"Yes." Ozma looked back down the long, empty stretch of the throne room. "Me, neither."

THE EMERALD CITY had never looked more gloriously radiant, but that was to be expected. Bungle had only previously graced it with her ordinary, extraordinary presence. Now that she was newly enlightened...

Trotting along Central Avenue toward the main gate, she couldn't feel anything but pity for the poor fools on every side, trudging about their days selling each other bread and milk, laughing at their exchanges of mindless frivolity, possessing no understanding at all of the truth. The world they inhabited closed about them like a palisade wall, a barrier that the merest sort of effort would overcome, but could they be bothered to make that effort?

No, they could not.

At the gate, she kept her nose in the air and didn't bother

acknowledging the Soldier with the Green Whiskers when he tipped his hat and said, "Good afternoon, Bungle." Outside the gate, she merely sniffed when Jellia Jamb called, "Don't be late for supper tonight, Bungle. The Royal Chefs're making cheese chowder!" And a hundred yards down the Yellow Brick Road, she only stumbled about half a step at the sight of Glinda herself seated in her usual white robe upon a golden chair among the field of flowers off to the right, the tips of her fingers pressed together and her gaze focused solely upon Bungle.

She considered arching her back and hissing, but no. *Let the witch watch,* Bungle thought, flicking her whiskers into a feline chuckle at the word play. After all, she'd found the dusty old books atop one of Glinda's bookcases after climbing it in her ongoing quest to find napping spots that wouldn't get her sideways glances and grouchily muttered comments. Most likely, the witch had placed the tomes there in an attempt to hide their contents from anyone enterprising enough to take advantage of them. But of course, she hadn't accounted for Bungle.

Not that Bungle normally cared much for books, but these had had a scent about them, a clear, flowing-water freshness that belied their mold-bedecked outer coverings. And what she'd found inside—the truth about Oz and its place in the literary and actual universe as well as the spell for leaving this realm of never-ending, never-aging, never-changing tedium— the books had opened Bungle's eyes in ways she was certain Glinda had sought to prevent.

At first, she'd thought that Ozma had to be involved in the conspiracy as well, but Her Majesty's reactions in the throne room just now had convinced Bungle of her innocence. Doubtless the so-called good witch had played upon the young monarch's credulity when briefing her about the alleged dangers of the public domain. But when faced with someone truly stalwart, Ozma had bowed to the inevitable despite whatever dire warnings Glinda may have planted in her ears.

It seemed only fitting, therefore, that Glinda witness Bungle's triumph.

The spell had claimed that it would only work in areas with unobstructed views of the earth and sky, and the grassy, flower-strewn flatland between the city and the forest certainly met that criterion. So Bungle stopped, glanced back at Glinda, spoke the words, performed the gestures, and stared at the suddenly fuzzy spot that appeared in the air before her.

Not knowing what to expect, she spread her whiskers, readied herself to spin in case she began to fall and to slash in case she was beset by the actual humans the books said inhabited the Reading World. Ears perked and eyes wide, she hopped through—

And found herself in a deep, dark stretch of woodland.

Bungle glanced quickly around. It didn't in fact look much different from the woods between Munchkinland and the Emerald City. Perhaps the branches overhead and the roots beneath her paws stretched themselves along in a more tangled fashion, the tree trunks a bit mossier and more bulging, the air heavier with the scent of rotting vegetation, the breeze a bit cooler and damper than she liked.

But why the silence? The books had gone into great and gloriously lurid detail about the automobiles honking and guns firing and machinery grinding that the Reading World abounded in! She'd expected jabbering mobs of furless bipeds lurching about, barely avoiding collisions with each other and nearly stomping on her tail! Where were the explosions and the shouting and the airships crashing and the—?

"By my ears and whiskers!" a pleasant purr of a voice said behind her. "To coin a phrase..."

Turning, Bungle saw a pair of unmistakably feline eyes and a set of grinning feline teeth regarding her from the shadow of a gnarled oak. "And yet," she said, peering more closely at the shadow, "by my own ears and whiskers, you have neither."

The grin widened. "Well, you can't have everything." A large feline shape began darkening the empty space around the eyes and teeth until an actual cat sat there looking back at her. "Where would you put it, for starters?"

Now that she could see the cat, Bungle wished that he'd stayed invisible. Large and ungainly, he looked more like a creature stitched into the shape of a cat from leftover bits and pieces of other animals, and Bungle found herself fervently wishing that he wouldn't prove to be as annoying as Scraps, the *other* patchwork person of her acquaintance. "So where are we?" she asked, hoping for a straightforward answer.

"Here." The cat, still grinning, patted the ground in front of him. "Or rather, *I'm* here." He lifted his paw and waved it vaguely in Bungle's direction. "*You're* over *there.*"

"And yet?" Turning, Bungle began marching away through the woods. "If you look *very* carefully, I think what you'll in fact discover is that"—she pronounced the next three words slowly and distinctly, snapping her tail with each one—"I am gone."

Leaving him quickly behind, she glared at the trees surrounding her for any sign of the Reading World. The books, after all, had promised her a place of shabby, secret, concrete alleyways and buildings that metaphorically scraped the sky. Obviously something had gone awry, so she needed to find an open spot where she could try casting the spell again.

The gray light beside her flickered and puffed into that same big, ungainly cat. "Such atrocious manners you have!" he said, his grin unfaded. "Aren't you going to ask my name?"

Bungle sighed. "Why would I care?"

"Excellent!" He walked with an odd rocking motion, both his right legs moving forward, then both his left legs. "You're halfway to becoming one of us!"

She gave him a sidelong glance. "And why would I want to do that?"

"He gave her that same abominable grin."

He gave her that same abominable grin. "Now you're three-fifths of the way." His tail flicked to tap Bungle's back. "You were correct in stating that you shouldn't care about my name since no one worth knowing here has anything but a title. Titles, after all, show how important one is. I'm the Cheshire Cat, and we shall call you the Glass Cat."

If her fur had been able to bristle, it would've been doing so. "I'm *already* called the Glass Cat," she got out through clenched teeth.

"How fortuitous!" His voice was still by far the best part of him, but Bungle found that it was becoming more grating by the moment. "Then you're three-quarters of the way to arriving here from your current state of there!"

"And yet?" She didn't even try to keep her ears up. "I'm not at all interested in being here! I'm interested in the real world, the Reading World beyond the public domain, the world from which all other worlds are sprung! Not some turgid, dull, and dreary woods!"

"Tulgey," the Cheshire Cat said. "Anyone clever will tell you that's the word you want, so I'm not surprised you're unfamiliar with it." His unusual gait became a strut. "Also, we made it up here ourselves."

And that, Bungle was about to announce with multiple claws against the side of his fat, bloated face, was enough of that. But before she could do more than stop and glare at him, a loud snuffling, snorting, and stomping began in the twilight of the tree canopy ahead. It sounded like a large creature, Bungle thought, and sniffing the air brought a more disturbing note to the rotting vegetation smell: rotting meat.

To advance seemed foolhardy, and as much as she hated to admit it, this Cheshire Cat was her only source of information. "Is that friend or foe approaching?" she murmured.

"Why, foe, of course," he announced as jovially as ever.

Bungle snapped her head in his direction, and the ruby in

her chest pounded to see that most of him had gone, only his infernal grin remaining. "It's your final test," the grin said. "To truly become one hundred percent here, you must slay the Jabberwock."

The roar that followed blasted a wave of charnel stench over her so thickly, she could feel it spatter her beautiful clearness. The force of it staggered her, though it did have the positive effect of blowing away every trace of the Cheshire Cat. Regaining her footing in the muddy, mossy dirt took more effort than she would've liked, and by then something enormously tall and thin, all arms and legs and bat-like flapping wings, had lurched from behind a tree to tower over her.

She stared up at what she assumed to be the Jabberwock. It stared down at her. Then, with much flexing of toe and finger claws, its snaky neck lashed out in her direction, the bulbous head on the end of it roaring again, its giant, peculiarly rectangular teeth spread wide and plunging rapidly nearer.

Without allowing herself to think, Bungle leaped straight into the creature's mouth, dug her claws into its tongue, and scrambled for the back of its throat.

Fortunately, its roar choked off almost at once: the sound, the stink, and the spray of it had already become tiresome. Dashing past the beast's inner teeth before circumstances could show her whether they were strong enough to shatter solid glass, Bungle didn't pause, leaped the abyss of its gullet, and slashed into the foul flesh of its upper esophagus.

Hot, sticky fluid drenched her, but as she'd suspected, the monster's thin neck proved to be its undoing. Bungle's claws tore straight through the sinewy tissue, and almost before she realized it, she was tumbling out into empty air. Behind her, the Jabberwock bubbled and reeled and writhed before collapsing into a nearly headless heap that at least cushioned her fall when she dropped onto it.

Blessed silence reigned for a moment, then a voice sang out, "Oh, frabjous day! Callooh! Callay!"

Peering through the horrid redness encrusting her vision, Bungle saw the Cheshire Cat stretched grinning along the bough of a nearby tree. "Listen carefully," he said, "and you'll next hear a sound that can only be described as 'chortling.'"

For an instant, she considered reacting in an uncouth fashion. But instead, she pressed the pads of one forepaw to the red stone around her neck and let herself concentrate on the sweet fragrance of the palace, on its many sunbeams and padded little nooks, on Ozma's lovely face.

A hum rang through her glass, and a puff of clean air—and more interestingly, a puff of clean light—shivered over her. The woods whisked away like a morning fog, and Bungle's next breath smelled the way it was *supposed* to smell, everything around her properly green-tinted and warm.

"BUNGLE!" Ozma sprang from her throne, dismay filling her at the sight of the Glass Cat dripping with reddish, brownish goo. "Guards! We need fresh towels here at once!"

Not waiting for them, she swooped down upon Bungle, bundled her into the trailing ends of her gown, and began wiping the filth away as best she could. "Are you all right? What happened? Why did you return so quickly? Was it truly awful?"

"It was... disheartening," Bungle said, but that she wasn't fussing or hissing or trying to wriggle free told Ozma a great deal more than the cat's words did. "I'm fairly certain I didn't reach the Reading World, but the place I went to, well, I'd rather not return there."

"Indeed," came a very familiar contralto voice.

"Glinda!" Jack Pumpkinhead called, and Ozma looked over to see Glinda the Good herself reclining on a gold-embroidered sofa that only appeared in that part of the room whenever the sorceress visited. "You're just in time for supper!" Jack continued. "Jellia Jamb's making cheese chowder!"

Glinda inclined her head toward Jack. "I happily accept your invitation." She shifted her smile, and Ozma as always thought of a lake, its placid surface giving no hint about what currents might be running beneath. "The public domain is a wild and unpredictable place, Bungle, and very few are those who find their way through it to the Reading World beyond."

Bungle's ears perked under Ozma's ministrations. "I find it interesting, witch, that you didn't say 'few are *we* who find our way through.'"

"Alas." Glinda sighed, and even though Ozma was very carefully not looking at her, she could nonetheless feel the sorceress's gaze like an itch along the side of her face. "I've been forbidden from making the attempt."

"Forbidden?" Bungle went still, then her wide eyes turned toward Ozma's. "It *is* you behind the cover-up. You've been to the Reading World, and you want no others to know the truth."

"Bungle," Ozma began, though she really had no idea what she was going to say next.

Thankfully, the glass cat's squirming interrupted her, and Ozma once again let her go, let her spin away to thump her paws onto the throne room carpet. "How could you?" Bungle spat. "I trusted you!"

"Please!" Holding up her stained gown in one hand, Ozma waved the other at Bungle, the cat's glass still befouled with blood and mud and who knew what else. "You've seen for yourself how horrid it is out there! And you got nowhere near the Reading World! Didn't you say that?"

"In fact," Glinda said, her tone as measured as always, "looking at the outlines of the spell—" Pages crinkled, and Ozma glanced over to see the sorceress leafing through a large and grimy book that had appeared in her lap. "I feel certain that you entered not only another fictional realm but also a fictional work within that fictional realm: a piece of writing read by one of the characters." She looked up, her smile placid. "The parameters here are apparently designed to send the caster in entirely the wrong direction to reach the Reading World."

Bungle's eyes widened, then narrowed. "I find myself wondering who exactly constructed that spell."

Glinda shrugged. "A large number of the books in my library are the sort for which proper provenance simply cannot be established."

"Fine." Bungle turned for the throne room doors. "It's the only spell I've got, however, so I'll just have to try it again, won't I?"

"Wait!" The word tore out of Ozma, ripped away scabs and sliced freshly along the tracks of long-knitted scars. "Please, Bungle! We... we'll come with you if you'll just... just wait!"

The cat paused, and Ozma almost sobbed with relief, not letting herself think about what she'd just said. As long as Bungle didn't leave...

A clattering beside her, and something as light as the uppermost branch of a tree draped itself across her back. "Father?" Jack asked, his voice close to her ear and unusually quiet. "Hunger has obviously overcome you. But fear not! It's very nearly supper time!"

For all that it wasn't funny, Ozma had to laugh, had to wrap her arms around the pumpkinhead's narrow frame and press her face into his green coat.

At that moment, footsteps thundered outside the throne room, courtiers rushing in with steaming, jade-colored towels. Furious scrubbing commenced, and after a remarkably brief time, Bungle, Ozma's gown, and the spots on the carpet had resumed their regular tints and lusters.

The attendants bowed themselves out, and Ozma, seated

once more upon her throne, finally let her gaze meet that of the Glass Cat, her nearly transparent tail curled about her paws. "You were saying?" Bungle asked into the sudden silence.

Glinda laughed and stretched. "Yes. You've got me all interested now."

And if Glinda's smile made Ozma sweat, the sorceress's laugh made her wish she could've spent the entirety of her life as an ignorant boy named Tip.

An impossibility, of course, and Ozma's sigh felt as though it were coming up from her ankles. "When Oz first entered the public domain, I took it upon myself to investigate it and the Reading World beyond." She couldn't stop a shiver, but she managed to keep the memories from flooding her. "I didn't care for it, and I forbade the only other one of my subjects who possessed the ability to visit from doing so." She nodded to Glinda. "Enforcing this order, however, has been a task I would describe with the phrase 'tiger by the tail.'"

Ozma then beheld the rarest of sights: her friend, mentor, and confidante blushing. "Still," Ozma went on, breathing in and breathing out, "now that a *second* feline's involved, it might in fact be best to... to make a proper expedition." She closed her eyes. "I can neither stop the clock from ticking, nor can I let fear rule my life. And for showing me that, I thank you both."

Opening her eyes, she let her temper rise a bit. "But I don't much appreciate being manipulated this way by my most trusted advisor." She shot Glinda a sharper glance. "Or would you have me believe that Bungle just happened to stumble upon the exact set of books necessary to set this chain of events into motion?"

Glinda's smile revealed nothing, of course.

But Bungle gave a loud snort. "I'm inclined to call it happenstance. A truly clever witch, after all, would've arranged for this to have happened much earlier."

"Earlier?" Jack started in his seat. "But then we'd have to wait that much longer for supper!"

Her tail switching, Bungle glared. "It's most annoying, the way you continue harping so loudly about supper! For you're no more able to eat than I am!"

Again, Ozma felt most keenly the pumpkinhead's inability to blink. "But everyone's together chatting at supper!" he said. "And that makes it the loveliest time of any day!"

Standing, Ozma caught Jack by the hand. "Very true, my friend." She reached her other hand out to Glinda and couldn't help beaming when the sorceress rose, stepped over, and took it. "One might also be tempted to observe, especially in light of Bungle's recent experience, that there's no place like—"

She let Bungle's hiss cut her off. "Finish that sentence," the Glass Cat said, brandishing her claws, "and I shan't be responsible for my actions." Her nose in the air and her tail aloft like a flag, Bungle began marching away along the grass-colored carpet.

Ozma laughed, and the thought occurred to her that the mistake she'd made the last time she'd ventured into the public domain and beyond was going alone. Nodding to the sorceress on one side and the pumpkinhead on the other, she followed Bungle out of the throne room and toward the dining room.

GO ON, LICK ME

LUNA CORBDEN

I am a toad. And I want you to lick me.

Your tongue won't hurt me at all. It's wide and rough and relatively short, but it will only tickle. I promise.

You think I'm merely an animal (you'd be wrong about that), not even a very smart animal, a fat round reptile (you'd be wrong about that, too), just out to catch flies from my hollow next to the desert river.

Come on, have a lick. You're not doing it for the flavor. I've never tasted myself but judging from the looks on people's faces, I'm not that great.

You know why you're here.

That's it. Draw me closer. You want to get the milky stuff leaking from my throat.

You've done worse—swallowed five spiders in your sleep, for instance. And that cold medicine your mom used to force on you. Don't get me started on that new health drink. I'm sure I taste better than that.

Or maybe not.

You won't know until you try. You can do it.

See that was pretty easy. Don't worry about me. Now just close your eyes. This is the best part.

Colors dance before you. If your eyes were open—hey I said close them! If your eyes were open, everything might shift a little, off the rails, under the sideways. Vertical lines might seem to bend. Shapes distort. That boulder you're looking at might twist into a knot.

It's like staring a little too long at an optical illusion, isn't it?

But now your eyes are closed. Not because I told you to. You can't understand this nonsensical croaking any more than I can interpret your mammalian blabbing. You've closed your eyes because the twisting trees and the unnatural tilt of the sky made you dizzy.

I tried to warn you.

You immerse yourself in this experience, watching the abstract colors as they rollick across the backside of your eyelids. Time distorts now. You have one epiphany after another.

You think it's a hallucination. I know better.

Have you ever seen the inside of another creature's subconscious? Have you ever seen inside *yours*?

No, you haven't. You're too afraid to look. You are so terrified of your own mind that you do crazy things like travel across the country to consume amphibian-secreted "hallucinogens". You do it for kicks. Maybe you delude yourself, saying you're here on a spiritual journey. Either way, you're unwilling to look at your own soul.

So instead, you unwittingly look into mine.

I smile at you with my wide mouth as your unsteady hand sets me back down under a dying scrub at the edge of the river. I squat on a crunchy brown leaf with my green toes curled around a fallen branch.

I could jump away in mock terror at being lifted into the air —and *licked*—by a giant. But I don't.

Because I've been waiting for this. I've been waiting for you. I've been waiting for this communion.

As your mind mingles with my soul and tastes my vivid and colorful perceptions, my psyche frolics with yours. The high you experience is nothing compared to my ecstasy. Your pretense may be spiritual pilgrimage, yet you know nothing of the transcendence I feel.

I hop among the lily pads of your personas, those you show your parents, those you show your friends, those you show your lover, those you show yourself, and those you hide from even yourself. I submerse myself in your ideas, your dreams and aspirations, art you've never bothered to create, deep thoughts you've never had the courage to express.

I catalog them, in sequence, an index of human thought. And then I begin dissecting. As a specimen, you are like every human. There is your heart, your brain, your gut, your nervous system. Your emotional organs are laid bare under my microscope.

Mentally, I sketch. The data is transmitted and recorded forever.

After a half hour, your high wears off. My connection to you grows thin and snaps. I leap off the branch and sink slowly into the still, murky water. My eyes peek above the surface as you stumble off with declarations like, "Whoa man!" and "What a trip!"

You get back on your mountain bike or hop into your jeep, whooping it up with your friends or waxing long and mellow about your amazing spiritual connection to nature, or the divine in all things, or some claptrap nonsense. You think your life is changed.

You don't even look back at me, and you will never pay me any mind. I am just a frog that secretes psychoactive chemicals.

And you are just an intriguing life form with several interesting talents.

Having much of a clue is not one of them.

NINE WAYS TO THEN

DIANA A. HART

My paws pounded against the carpet, a furious thunder that matched the drumming of my heart. A meowl tore from my throat. I dropped flat, claws digging into the fiber, and lashed my tail as the visions hit me again. My pupils dilated. Nine versions of reality poured into my skull and smothered my senses, each a fluttering glimpse of what could be.

Clara, my master, stood in line at the student café. In each vision she wore her backpack and clutched a travel mug covered in prancing reindeer. Fingerless mittens—the ones that made her hands look like funny little paws—curled around the warm plastic as she waited for her order. I felt the ache in her belly. The way the aromas of fresh bread and cooking meat made her mouth water. My whiskers twitched in shared hunger. True, not as appetizing as freshly mangled pigeon, but at least she shared my love of bacon.

A man with dog-brown eyes smiled at her. My fur puffed. Something in his gaze was cold. Calculating. Like the neighbor's calico when she stared at the bird feeder. Dog-Eyes stalked closer and complimented Clara's pink scarf. Causality scattered like a flock of sparrows. My mind could only keep track of the nine most stable, tumbling through dinners that hadn't yet happened, walks and talks and movies they hadn't shared yet—some they wouldn't, depending how chaos fluttered—but in the end they all settled in the same place: beatings. Crying. Silence. The kind my visions couldn't pierce...

Anguish exploded from my throat. "No!" I tore into the darkened living room. Streetlight poured through frost-covered windows, casting fractal shadows across the floor. *There has to be a way to stop it!* "How?" I yowled and bounded over the couch, muscles screaming with the need to move, to do something, anything, to change the way the future fluttered. "How!?" The television remote clattered under my paws. Thumped to the floor.

"Dang it, Bixby," Clara moaned from the bedroom. "It's three in the morning."

Three in the morning... I skidded to a halt. *Morning! Yes!* Whiskers thrumming, I sank into a crouch. Thoughts churned so fast my fur twitched. The visions always started close to the present. Whatever morning I'd seen, it'd happen soon. My ears flattened. I just had to figure out when it was and stop Clara from meeting Dog-Eyes.

Contemplative churrs rolled off my tongue as I picked through the visions, looking for clues. Clara grumped again from the bedroom. I tuned her out. Focused only on the future: her backpack and her coffee mug, how hungry she was for breakfast, the way her scarf—

I froze. *It's pink.* Bile rose in my throat. *She laid that one out tonight!* My heart leapt to a gallop. I cried out and thundered to her door.

Closed. "No!" I reached up for the knob. Brass slid between my paws, too slick for me to accomplish more than a soft rattle of metal. I flopped on my side and stuck my legs beneath the door. Waved them about and called to Clara. Plaintive cries bore no fruit. Blankets rustled behind the faux wood panel and I caught the soft floomph of Clara pulling her pillow over her head.

I pressed my nose to the gap. Reached even further under the door. *I will save you.* My paws found only open air.

SOMEWHERE AROUND DAWN Clara stumbled to the bathroom and left her bedroom door open. I waited until I heard the splash of water before slinking into her room, a dead mouse dangling from my jaws. Christmas lights winked along the ceiling, casting a dim but cheery glow, and the first blush of sun crept up her plank-and-milk-crate bookshelf. Tail cocked, I padded to the chair in the corner. Clara's outfit—a long gray skirt, wool sweater, and a bunny-soft pink scarf—spilled over the seat. I hopped onto the cushion and proceeded to chew the mouse into pieces.

As I sprinkled meat and offal across her scarf I felt a small pang of guilt. Not for the mouse of course—this particular vermin would have pooped in the pancake mix next week—but rather for Clara. Whenever she found one of my kills she'd make a funny grunt and shake like somebody had dripped water on her nose. *Still, it's for your own good.* I plopped the last chunk of leg down.

Causality shifted. Churned just past my whisker-tips. I couldn't see where reality fluttered yet, but something had changed. Across the hall water flushed. I licked my lips, coppery blood sharp on my tongue, and hopped off the chair.

Clara padded back into the room, yawning. Her dark hair was mussed from sleep and she rubbed a palm against her eye. "Hey fuzz-butt."

I chirped a good morning and twined about her legs. With a sleepy chuckle she slid back under the covers, no doubt trying to catch a bit more sleep before her alarm started screeching. She pulled the blankets up and scratched the comforter in invitation. I just stared. Agitation thrummed through me, made my tail twitch. My visions were still a vague hum that buzzed against my whiskers and until they cleared I didn't know if Clara was safe. She scratched the blankets again, murmuring for me. A chill raced up my spine. I told myself it was just the cold and hopped onto the bed.

Fiberfill muffled my footsteps. Pressing against her hand, I enjoyed a few luxurious strokes before I curled my tail around my paws and sank into a puddle of fur. Clara smiled and drifted back to sleep. Her fingers splayed across the blankets, barely brushing my coat. Chaos spread from her touch, stirring my fur like a snake in the grass, but it refused to resolve.

I oozed closer. Pressed my nose up next to hers and breathed in her spent air. Traces of last night's dinner, butter and pasta with a bit of pepper, still clung to her breath. My throat tightened. *Please, let it have worked.* I pulled in a deeper breath. Sniffed at her eye. All that came of it was a sleepy grimace.

I settled back onto the blanket. Maybe this was a good sign. Perhaps the visions had stopped because Dog-Eyes wouldn't notice her now. Satisfaction lured me into a slow blink. Minutes slipped by as I watched Clara sleep, her round, soft features free of bruises. Warm as the day she'd found me shivering under a shopping cart. *And nobody will take that away.* I closed my eyes and began to purr.

Sharp squeals split the air. I jerked, popping out of dreams I hadn't realized I'd fallen into. Clara groaned and slapped the clock. Shivered as she kicked off the blankets and headed for her clothes. I dropped to the floor, chirping. Everything was normal. I wouldn't have been able to sleep if—

A familiar grunt hit my ears. Causality began to churn.

I stopped, tail-tip twitching.

"Really?" Clara said. She picked up her scarf by the ends, shuddered, and held it at arm's length as she headed for the trashcan. The nebulous churn turned to nine points of pressure. I stiffened. Mouse-bits tumbled into the can as the future crashed over me. Causality battered my vision like a flock of sparrows, then and now a fluttering, chaotic mess.

My pupils went wide. Same café, same backpack, same mug... Now-Clara flicked her pink scarf into the laundry. Shivers raced up my spine, arching my body. In my visions Dog-Eyes walked up to then-Clara and commented on her blue, tasseled scarf. Now-Clara pulled matching fabric out of her dresser. My throat squeezed too tight to screech.

I burst into motion, thundering down the hallway.

"Ugh, I should have printed this off last night," Clara said from the living room. I paused, mouth full of food, and flicked an ear her direction. Brewing coffee and fresh ink reached my nose. There was a smack of palm-on-plastic. "Come on, work!" Paper crumpled as the printer ate another page of Clara's essay. She made a noise somewhere between a whimper and a growl.

In the bathroom I sighed and crunched down more tuna-scented kibble, hoping it would quiet my stomach. Trying to save Clara had left me with sore muscles and a belly full of acid. She was trickier than the red dot, foiling every attempt to keep her from meeting with Dog-Eyes. Laying in the sink so she couldn't brush her teeth? Countered with a scoop and a plop. Hair ball in the kitchen? Paper towels and Windex. Sitting on her cell phone so she couldn't find it? Clara just called it from the land-line. My tail twitched. Granted, the butt-massage had been fantastic, but my visions remained unchanged.

A whoop burst from the living room. "Finally!"

My fur puffed. *You're almost out of time!* I choked down the last bit of breakfast—leaving a ring of garnish behind, of course—and hurried for Clara.

"Late, late, late," she chanted, shoving her essay into her bookbag. The computer gave a good-bye ding and went black. She snatched up her bag, halfway zipped, and hurried for the kitchen. I followed after, hounded by the flutter of what would soon be.

Clara tossed her bag on the floor by the coffeemaker and trotted to the dishwasher. Oozing around the door frame, I rubbed my cheek against the stove and gave my tail a little jiggle. Did my best to act calm. Inside I was yowling. *Think!* The dish-rack clattered. My whiskers twitched, heavy with fast-approaching reality. Clara cursed and pushed the dishwasher shut. Her feet slapped softly against the linoleum as she bounded for the cabinets. I perked, a new plan flash-forming.

While Clara dug her travel mug out of the cupboard I tossed myself on the floor behind her. She turned around, kicking me in the side as I rolled onto my back. Pain lanced my ribs.

"Augh, Bixby!" she yelped, breaking into an awkward stagger. Her other foot thumped down near my head. My pulse spiked. She gaped at me, eyes wide. "You okay?"

Not really, but I just pulled my paws up under my chin. Curled into a C-shape that fluffed my belly fur. "Now?" I chirped.

She frowned. Reached down and rubbed under my chin. "Sorry, buddy," she said and began to straighten.

"No!" I rolled forward, pawing after her bare hand. Clara headed for the coffee pot. Claws scrabbling at the linoleum, I got in front of her again and flopped across her path, rolling about and purring a loud as I could. "Now?" *Please, let it work.* "N-n-now?" Clara pursed her lips. I chirped.

Clicking her tongue, she crouched down and started rubbing the fur on my belly. Pure joy rang through me, a belltoll of warmth that flooded my blood and bones. My purrs went from rumble to ear-rattling-quake.

The sparrow-flutter of causality twanged my whiskers. Rolled across my senses. Two of the nine visions replaced the café and Dog-Eyes with Clara's car, chuggy engine rumbling as she sped for college. My eyes closed in rapture. *It's working!* A third vision began to blur away from Dog-Eyes, twisting slowly into icy highway. *Just a few minutes more...*

In my skull a semi's horn blared. Then-Clara whipped her head around. All she saw was chrome. Glass exploded. Steel squealed. Pain and silence followed.

My eyes snapped open. *Oh hairballs no!* Desperate, I sunk claws and teeth into flesh. The new visions flapped in my head, twisting steel and the scream of angry jays, as Clara yelped and pulled back. Blood beaded from several scratches. I leapt onto the kitchen counter, ribs throbbing and fur twitching with stress. Great sweeps of my tail betrayed my agitation. I stared off into nothing and tracked the visions. *Don't be locked in.* Reality beat at me. Battered me as the three altered threads flailed about, seeking the strongest path. *Don't come true.*

Clara shook her hand. Hissed over her wrist and shot me a glare. I hardly noticed. Mangled steel and burnt rubber morphed back to crisping bacon and predatory brown eyes. A shiver started in my belly and shot up my back, traveling into my paw. I gave it a few quick flicks. Licked it, as much to quiet my nerves as to wipe away the tang of Clara's blood.

Grumbling, Clara popped the lid off her travel mug and filled it with steaming coffee. Prancing cartoon reindeer grinned up at me, beaming at my ineptitude. Shame made my neck smolder. I stared out the frosty window. Watched a cardinal toss millet out of the feeder to get at the sunflower seeds. It only made me think of Dog-Eyes. I chirped a curse.

"Dang it," Clara said looking at her wrist again. She replaced the coffee pot, snapped the lid on her mug, and set it on the edge of the counter. "Nice work, fuzz-butt." She tried to stroke my shoulders as she breezed towards the bathroom. Ashamed, I ducked under her touch. I didn't deserve her if I couldn't save her. A few moments later the medicine cabinet clinked shut. Paper ripped as Clara put on a few Band-Aids.

My nose wrinkled. *What else can I do?* Clara tromped to the front door. I snuck a glance over my shoulder. She pulled on a pair of orange and pink socks, followed by puffy snow boots. The fingerless mittens were next. I gulped. There had to be something left. *Get hit by a car?* It could work, but was I willing to do that? Dash out the door when she opened it, mangle myself and maybe die so that she wouldn't meet Dog-Eyes? *And what if that just makes things worse...*

Clara wrapped the blue scarf around her neck. Nine times over I heard Dog-Eyes compliment it. Then the tumbling flutter of their intertwined lives, followed by crying, pain, and silence. Nine hollow futures roared in my skull. My stomach knotted.

Clara cast about for her keys. It wouldn't take her long to figure out I'd knocked them behind the couch this morning. Ears flat, I took a fortifying breath and turned to face the door.

Out of the corner of my eye prancing reindeer grinned at me. My breath caught. *Her coffee.* Spider-hunting slow, I glanced at the mug. Peered over the counter. She'd dropped her bag next to the coffee pot, gaping half-open where she'd left it. Her essay peeked out from between a pair of textbooks.

Clara oofed. Keys jingled.

My head snapped up. Clara strode for the kitchen. What could be surged around me like wing-beats, unrelenting. Blood pounded in my ears. I sidled closer to her reindeer mug. Lifted my paw. Something in the way I moved caught Clara's attention. Her eyes went wide.

She sucked in a breath. "Don't you da—"

I slapped a reindeer right in his shiny red nose. The travel mug flopped over, glugging merrily, and rolled off the counter into her bag. Clara yowled and broke into a run. I just stared over the edge of the counter, head cocked. Brown liquid poured over her belongings. Dog-Eyes and the café burst away like terrified finches. I wasn't quite sure where they were headed, but I could feel the distance growing, leaving Dog-Eyes far behind. I sat up straighter, smirking as only a cat could.

Clara dragged the sopping remains of her essay out of her bag. She glared up at me. "You're an asshole."

I just chirped and tossed my head.

Cussing, she yanked her books out of her bag, shook the worst of the coffee off over the sink, and tossed them on the counter before stomping into the living room. A happy little chime told me she'd turned on her computer.

Sparrow wings brushed across my senses. My pupils widened. Each vision settled to roost. Three then-Claras got breakfast after lecture, two fell asleep in class. Another three skipped out and went their separate ways around town. The last then-Clara slapped the printer, gave up on her essay, and crawled back in bed. Then-me joined her not long after.

I blinked in slow contentment. There was no telling which then-Clara now-Clara would become, but for now they were safe. *I hope she picks the last one.* Either way, I closed my eyes and purred.

TOAD'S GRAND BIRTHDAY EXTRAVAGANZA

LENA NG

There is nothing so joyous as the snow melts away, and the early green buds burst from the branches, and the sun grows stronger and brighter, and the winter's chill departs from your bones, and the vibrant colours of Easter flowers and emerald grass begin to paint the land—as a heavy, hearty, welcome-to-a-new-spring breakfast. So thought Mole as he stretched and yawned, and stretched and yawned again, belly up under a blue-and-white quilt, while the perfume of spring seeped into his cozy, underground abode.

Soon the smell of sputtering bacon and button mushrooms, reheated tinned beans, roasting tomatoes, fried potatoes, and fresh coffee, mingled and danced and filled the air in his kitchen. So many lovely smells, delicious smells, that it didn't take long before a rap sounded at his front door.

Mole set down two big plates of blue earthenware on his round wooden table. "Door's open," he called out. A pointed, curious nose found its way through the front door and down the underground hallway to the kitchen. The whiskers on this snout twitched and shiny nostrils flared with all the smelling of the food cooking on the speckled blue, pot-bellied stove.

"Ratty," said Mole, scooping a generous helping of baked beans onto each plate, "I was hoping you would join me. Welcome, welcome spring!"

"Glorious spring," agreed Rat. "And even better with a full stomach." He helped with pouring the coffee and getting out the knives and forks. The past winter had seemed especially long and especially cold, and although his house on the river bank was lined with mud to keep out the draft, there was nothing like a good dose of sunlight after the dismal grey. And to see the river thawing from slow and sluggish to leaping and alive delighted Rat every year. "I was on the way back from gathering supplies—for fishing and the like, talking lure-craft and river lore and that sort of thing—when those marvellous smells told me you were awake." Animals in general know it isn't proper form to disturb their hibernating kinsmen, just as you yourself would not appreciate being woken in the middle of the night from a deep, dreamless sleep. Instead there were ways to find out who was up-and-about: the grapevine of gossipy rabbits and informative hedgehogs; the sounds of spring-cleaning; run-ins at the market for seeds and herbs.

The tucking in was made even more delicious after the

winter's fast. The catch-up of news would be saved for after the sipping and slurping and crunching and savouring. At last, with his stomach stretching his plaid pyjamas to the table, Mole sat back with a contented sigh. "More coffee, Ratty?"

Rat leaned over his own stuffed stomach to inch his mug closer to the coffee pot. His belly was comfortably full and another cup of coffee would fill in all the small gaps.

Mole halted mid-pour as a low buzz filled the room. The buzz rattled the dishes on the table and stacked on the shelves. The sound faded and Mole started to pour again.

Buuuuzzzz. There it was again. It could be a buzz saw or a lawnmower or a low-flying two seater aircraft...

"Oh, no," said Rat as his nose twitched. He stared up at the packed-earth ceiling. "It can't be."

"Can't be what?" asked Mole.

"That Toad, Toad of Toad Hall, Toad of Complete and Utter Foolishness. What silly thing is he up to now?"

Despite his heavy stomach, Rat was quickly away from the table and through the underground hallway to the front door. Mole struggled to catch up.

"How do you know it's Toad?" Mole panted.

"Because anything strange or new or bizarre—it can only be him."

Rat flung the door open and they both squinted against the bright spring light as they made their way into the awakening field. The propeller's buzz started to grow louder as it swooped overhead. It was a snub-nosed, two-seater plane, painted a fire-hydrant red.

Mole's normally small black eyes grew wide on his sleek, ebony-furred face. Behind the pilot's goggles and wrapped with a red scarf waving in the wind was definitely Toad. Attached to the plane's back rudder was an enormous flapping banner reading:

TOAD'S GRAND BIRTHDAY EXTRAVAGANZA. TOMORROW 4 PM TOAD HALL.

Mole jumped up and down and waved his small paws. "Toad, over here, look down," he called out.

"Don't encourage him," said Rat as the plane buzzed out of sight. "Because of his jailbreak, he's still a wanted toad. He's supposed to be laying low. Instead he's inviting all of the wild wood to his party. No, this won't do. We'd better get Badger."

After the washing up and putting away the crockery, Mole changed into his hiking togs while Rat amassed the necessary supplies for a journey into the wild wood. There was no time to gather the prerequisite plants to carry in their pocket or to perform the safety rituals but they had their walking sticks which would likely serve them well if they met up with trouble.

The bright sunlight soon grew hidden by the trees as Mole and Rat made their way through the dense forest. The brush and crackle of beech leaves underfoot and the snap of small twigs and branches caused suspicious eyes to peer out at them through small holes in the tree trunks. At the sight of the sturdy walking sticks and two companions marching with purpose, these mistrustful eyes disappeared right back into their hideaways.

The friends trudged on in watchful silence until at last they saw the iron nameplate of Mr. Badger.

"Yes, I saw the banner," Badger said gruffly as they settled into their armchairs, with steaming cups of tea and small plates of sandwiches resting on the side tables to revive them. "The whole wood saw it, with the ruckus his plane was making. I'm surprised he's still flying it; I thought it was repossessed. Well, we'd better be off since I'm the only one who can talk any sense into him."

Badger led them back through the wild wood, down the hidden pathways and clandestine trails, cautious yet confident as always. He recited the essential passwords and gestured the required signals and soon they emerged from the dappled light of the dense forest into the open meadow leading to Toad Hall.

After some time trekking through bluebells and brambles, the ivy-covered stone facade of Toad Hall came into view. The snub-nosed plane sat in front of the west wing of the house, its owner waving as the companions drew closer.

"My dear, dear friends," Toad said, putting away the cloth after polishing the side of the red plane to a gleam. "I take it you've seen my invitation to my little soirée." With his goggles pushed back on his broad head and his pilot's uniform of a brown suede flying jacket with a shearling collar, red scarf tied nattily around his neck, Toad was the picture of dashing. "Thank-you, thank-you for helping me prepare for my birthday party. It will be the biggest, grandest party in existence. A special day where I would like to treat all of my friends. All to commemorate, well... me. I'm turning four." Four may seem young but it was a ripe, respectable age for any toad.

Mole examined the underside of the plane closely, mainly because his eyesight was poor, and he was very round and small and couldn't look much higher. Rat clambered up into the passenger side and leaned back into the leather seat. Although he was dedicated to his river, Rat decided he would write his next poem about flying.

Badger's stern look through his round spectacles didn't seem to damper Toad's enthusiasm. The grey whiskers on his cheeks quivered. "Don't let this party run wild, Toad. By not controlling the guest list, you don't know who will turn up. Remember the time your house was overrun with stoats and weasels."

"Hee, hee," Toad laughed. "Wasn't it a magnificent time running them off? Stoats and weasels had no defense against my mighty cudgel. A whoop and a sound licking and off they ran." A self-satisfied smile crossed his homely face. "But with the party, it's too late. I've invited everyone and I've spared no expense. There's champagne in the icebox, canapes and caviar, and gifts to take home. Now help me wrap the party favours."

Toad led them through the arched doorway of Toad Hall, down the portrait gallery of Toads Past to the grand dining room. In a gigantic mound on the polished herringbone floor were treats and enjoyments of every shape and size. There were beautifully painted books whose illustrations popped up from the page. When a tab was pulled, the cut-out horses with flowing painted manes would lope around a carousel or a lion would leap at the paper cage bars or a lark would open its beak and sing. There were boxes of striped sugar candy cubes which would fizz and snap in your mouth when you ate them. There were lavender recorders and pink whistles. There were foil pinwheels and contraptions which blew bubbles and yoyos and tin cars which raced around the room with the turning of a metal key. Pages could be written on the variety of enchantments lying on Toad's floor. It was all very delightful. It also looked like a lot of work to wrap them.

Before the grumbling could start, Toad held open his arms. "Please, my dear friends, I need your help. You're right, Badger, this party will get out of hand without your assistance. But it's my birthday and all I want to do is make others as happy as I am."

Well, no one could say no to that so Badger, Rat, and Mole spent the rest of the day and into the evening wrapping gifts while Toad sang rousing wild wood songs to keep their spirits going as he hung up the streamers and balloons.

THE NEXT DAY, the group had barely set upon their lavish breakfast—since, despite his faults, Toad was an excellent host and never did things by halves—before the doorbell began to chime. Over the morning, in streamed a parade of a musicians, caterers in liveried uniform, jugglers in bright costume, somersaulting clowns sporting fuzzy wigs, twirling ballerinas, and other entertainers.

A large, striped canopy with a stage for speeches was set up in Toad's back acreage. There were three tables for the food and drink. A small, fenced in area held the petting zoo with miniature ponies and pygmy goats. Another large table held the cheerfully-wrapped gifts for the guests. In the back, much to Badger's chagrin, was an enormous pile of fireworks.

"How much did all this cost?" Mole asked with mouth dropped open as he surveyed the party landscape. Toad Hall was set on five acres of green, fertile land with plenty of room for all of the celebration's amusements.

"Never mind," said Toad, proudly wearing his bespoke tailored birthday outfit. It was an orange suit with fashionably-thin lapels with a patch of the Toad Hall coat of arms sewn on the front, accompanied by a striped blue-and-orange silk bow tie. He also sported a splendid hat which could have put any royal hat to shame. "You only turn four once."

With all the coordinating and setting up—the tiered cake was to go here and the chocolate fountain would go there and the pyramid of champagne glasses were to be arranged over there—and Toad practicing his speech and songs, with some fine-tuning and editing by accomplished poet Rat, the time hurried by and soon it was four o'clock.

"Well, I'm off," said Badger, as the first guests, a dozen or so of rabbits, started to hop in. "Happy returns, dear Toad."

"You're not staying for the party?"

Badger packed his day bag with a few edibles for the road. "You know how much I hate society and parties. Peace and quiet is all I care for. But I promise to return tomorrow to help you with the cleaning up."

"We'll keep him out of trouble," said Rat. Mole nodded enthusiastically with a mouth full of pistachio pudding.

~

RAT AND MOLE had to agree. It *was* the grandest party in existence. The fireflies gave a twinkling, flirtatious light. The ballerinas pirouetted and the jugglers juggled and the edibles were eaten and the drinkables quaffed. Toad's larger-than-life presence lorded over everything.

And the noise! No polite party conversation here. Instead the happy cacophony of live music and snippets of carousing songs and excited chatter and laughter. Even Toad's terrible jokes seemed to be immensely funny, and it was his own booming laughter that was the loudest at the telling. Everyone admired Toad's flourishing hat and wished him happy returns, and the champagne flowed like the river.

A few weasels and stoats appeared, hats in hands, quite humbled by their previous defeat. Toad bore them no animosity since they sincerely wished him longevity and best wishes, and they joked a bit about their past scuffles and Toad's stalwart fighting. The Chief Weasel pledged his best behaviour and unwavering loyalty and brought an enormous wicker basket filled with aged cheeses, candied fruit, crystalized crickets and other such amphibian delicacies as a gift from them all.

Finally, a drum-roll sounded and a hush fell upon the celebrants. Toad ascended onto the stage. He stood for a few moments, soaking in the attention. "My dear, wonderful, considerate, kind—"

This went on for several minutes until all the appropriate adjectives were exhausted.

"—loyal, generous, loving friends," Toad began. "Thank-you for sharing my special day."

A cheer arose from the crowds.

Toad cleared his throat and waited for silence. "I suppose you are all wondering about the origins of Toad." After a pregnant pause, "It all began in the mid-thirteenth century, when my great ancestor, Toad de Bonaparte, was still a tadpole wriggling in a fish pond deep in the heart of France..." He regaled the crowd with the history of Toad and somehow managed to make it all the way to the beginning of the fifteenth century before someone yelled—

"Song!"

Which Toad didn't seem to mind since who could blame anyone for wanting to get to the good part. He changed his stance, breathed deeply with his diaphragm, and poured forth a self-composed song, sung mainly in key.

Just as Toad reached the highest note of his song, the stage began to rumble. Across the field sounded the pitter-patter of an army of little feet. Little feet running, little feet jumping, little feet racing down the hillside and over the green grass and heading directly towards Toad Hall. Hundreds of little feet belonging to a horde of...

Lemmings!

Lemmings, lemmings everywhere, pudgy brown fur balls from all over the countryside. They guzzled all the champagne. They cannonballed into the chocolate fountain, spraying founts of chocolate. They chittered all at once in their high-pitched voices so that no one could hear the sound of their own thoughts. They razed through the birthday cake and vacuumed up the canapes and hors d'oeuvres.

The party guests scattered. The miniature ponies and pygmy goats jumped the fence and ran off, booting lemmings left and right. Toad went into a manic panic of racing here and there but wasn't able to accomplish much of anything. The stoats and weasels sprang up at once and managed to gather a few of the lemmings under their arms but the sheer numbers overwhelmed them.

A piercing whistle whizzed through the lemming crowd. It ended in an explosion of heat, light, and colour. A stream of fireworks skyrocketed through the mass of Rodentia. A ringing bang and the lemmings were tossed about and tumbling.

Toad ran to the back where the fireworks were kept. There stood Badger, carefully setting off the missiles, his aim honed by his previous years in the military. "Badger, Badger, how did you know to return?" asked Toad, gasping.

"The lemmings had stormed the wild wood and I knew they would cause chaos," Badger replied, methodically aiming a Cherry Blaster and setting it alight. The lemmings scattered and scampered, run off by the screaming streams of swirling colour. A crazed excitement filled Toad and he began to set off the fireworks willy-nilly.

"Be careful," shouted Badger, "or you'll burn Toad Hall to the ground."

Caution or foresight were never parts of Toad's character, and he jumped onto the biggest firework in his arsenal.

"Get off of there!" Badger said.

But it was too late and Toad had set off the biggest firework while sitting right on it. Perched backwards, Toad jockeyed the Colossal Chrysanthemum as the firework shot into the sky. The big rocket exploded, ejecting Toad into the starry stratosphere in a burst of fiery confetti. Rat and Mole watched in open-mouthed, horrified awe as they saw a Toad-shaped figure silhouetted against the moon's bright face, one arm waving a massive hat.

But gravity gives no exception and toads who go up, must also come down. They heard a mighty thud and saw an eruption of coloured wrapping paper where Toad had landed.

Rat, Mole, and Badger ran to the landing spot. There they

found Toad collapsed under a pile of brightly-wrapped presents.

"Toad, oh Toad," said Mole, hands clasped together and with tears streaming from his liquid-black eyes. "Please tell us you're all right."

Toad opened one eye and then the other, looking up at three furrowed expressions. Face blackened from gunpowder, his belly started shaking from laughter. "Best birthday ever," Toad exclaimed, miraculously without the loss of a single tooth. "Let's do it again next year."

ISSUE 6

HIBERNATION

As winter melts into spring, readers and bears alike awake from their hibernation.

Emerge from your cave, dear reader-bear, look around, and see the stories we have for you to read!

Once you've seen these stories—full of dragons and bears; creatures gigantic and minuscule; voyages both out into the universe and inward to the truest self—feel free to withdraw into your cave and read them in deep, dark seclusion. But don't hoard them like a dragon, keeping the stories hidden forever in your cave.

After poring over this treasure trove of words, savoring them, and delighting in them, don't keep them only for yourself —share the treasure! Share our stories far and wide.

DRAGON CHILD

STELLA B. JAMES

From the mouth of my cave, I can see the destruction; thick pillars of smoke, almost black in color. I can hear the cries of many people, men and women alike. The villages are being pillaged, the castle under siege. I lay my head back down with a snort and close my eyes. Those silly humans have nothing better to do than allow their greed to consume them.

I hear her panting before I can spot her, and a man warning

her to fall back. They are more foolish than the humans down below. Who would dare enter my dwelling? I haven't bothered them in decades, why do they test me? I sit up on my haunches and give myself a shake, my wings spreading out behind me.

An aged woman falls to her knees at the mouth of the cave, clutching something to her chest. A man follows, a soldier from the look of his bloodied armor. I eye them with curiosity. It doesn't seem like they have come to challenge me. But they couldn't expect to seek refuge here either. What could have made them desperate enough to climb my mountain?

"Dragon." The woman gasps out the word, her breathing still labored, but it isn't spoken out of fear. No, it almost sounds like a plea. I straighten and glare down at her, letting a small stream of smoke dispel from my nostrils. She bows her head as the man wrenches her back to him, his hands clasping at her shoulders.

"It isn't safe here," he warns in a harsh whisper. I shake my head and chuckle in amusement. It isn't safe anywhere at the moment.

"I have come to ask you a favor!" the woman cries out to me, ignoring her male companion. I cock my head to the side. Now this is interesting. I've been demanded my riches, my magic, even my death. But never asked. I nod my head once and she continues, "The princess is all that has survived. You must protect her. She'll be our last hope."

My eyes survey the mouth of the cave, but I see no woman, or girl. I'm not sure how old this princess is supposed to be. The woman seems to understand my confusion. With outstretched arms, she places a bundled up cloth in between us. I eye it for a moment, and then glance back at the woman. I'm tempted to set her on fire for whatever trick she is trying to play. But then the bundle moves.

It wriggles this way and that until a little hand snakes out. The cloth falls away, revealing a tiny face and wide eyes the color of emeralds. The princess is but an infant. Smooth skin, soft flesh, and dark, wispy curls. How am I to protect such a scrawny creature? She has no fur to warm her, no scales or teeth to defend her. She doesn't even have wings to make her grand escapes.

The woman takes in my wide eyed caution and bows her head again with a barely audible *please* escaping her. I glance back down at the little creature, who simply waves her hands in the air as spit bubbles raspberry out of her mouth. With a grimace, I move my head down to inspect closer. The woman falls back on her bottom, the soldier having left her to jump in front of the swaddled youngling.

"You won't harm her!" he shrieks, brandishing his sword. I snarl down at him, letting him have a good look at my pointed teeth.

"Do others know you are here?" My voice comes out on a growl, and he takes a step back. The woman moves in front of him and shakes her head.

"No one saw us. I'm sure of it." Her hands clasp together in front of her, offering me her silent prayers. I close my eyes and sigh out in defeat.

"Flee from here and never return. I will keep the princess safe."

The soldier casts a worried glance towards the princess, and then back to me.

"And if they come for her?"

"They would be foolish to come here. But if such an event were to occur, I'd make sure they'd learn not to make the same mistake twice."

He nods his head at my answer and takes the woman by the hand. She allows him to drag her away, but before they are out of sight, she turns her wary eyes to me.

"Her name is Esmerelda."

They disappear and that is when the tiny being decides to

cry. I scrunch my eyes and flatten my ears best I can. I scoop her up in one claw and bring her closer. Her crying stops once she spots me, and her eyes shimmer with the remaining unshed tears. Her eyes are more beautiful than any jewel in my possession.

She wriggles herself free of the blankets and falls onto all fours. I snort in amusement as I watch her crawl in her clumsy way, much like a newborn dragon would. I don't know anything about humans or the way they grow. I know their hatred, their greed, and their violence. I know their screams, their terror, and their taste. But she is none of those things. She is still pure.

Her green eyes take me in, and she gurgles out some made up language I can't understand before her face breaks out into a smile. She reaches out to touch me, and I bring my snout close to her hand. My little princess is brave, that or completely foolish. Perhaps a little of both, but only time will tell.

"Oh, Esmerelda, what have I gotten myself into?"

SHE DOES this nearly every day. Her fingers grasp the lower branches, her feet find the rounded knobs. She pulls and pushes, grunts and gasps. She is getting faster now, her hands and feet having memorized the way. Her favorite branch sits thick and proud, swooping down where it meets the trunk.

She sits on the branch and scoots herself sideways toward the middle. I pretend to busy myself with my inner musings, but I'm aware of her every movement. Once she finds that perfect flat space of the branch, she moves to a crouch, and spreads her arms.

I hear her whisper, a small promise under her breath. *I can do this.* And in one swift movement, she pushes off from the branch. Her body sails into the air before bringing her back down. She doesn't have the sense to scream. My brave little fool fears nothing. I stretch out my wing to catch her, and she rolls into my side.

She grips my scales and climbs up to my back, her hands and feet having memorized this as well. She climbs to the top of my head and peeks over until her head is level with my eye. She bares her teeth at me and growls. I let loose my own growl, but she simply sticks her tongue out and slides down my snout. She balances herself on the very end, her legs dangling on either side, and sets her chin on my scales.

"When will I fly?" Another daily habit. Oh, how she wishes to fly. She loves my wings. Even after I have set her in the furs of her bed, I will wake up to find her curled up in the soft leather of my wings.

"When you grow wings."

She sighs, a small pout forming. "And when will that happen?"

"Maybe never. Not all dragons have wings."

She sits up, steadying herself by leaning forward on her small hands. "You said the same thing about scales and fire breathing."

I chuckle softly. She is quite inquisitive. "And it's true."

She slumps back down, the disappointment evident in her expression. "I make for a lousy dragon."

"You're the most beautiful there ever was." And this is the truest statement I've ever spoken. Her hair is like midnight, her eyes shine in their emerald glory, and her spirit is wild and stubborn. She is more dragon than I at times. And she is mine. *For the moment*, my mind whispers.

Four years have passed now, and no one has come to claim her. I doubt anyone would believe a little girl has survived in these mountains within the dragon's lair. I don't know if anyone would recognize her for who she truly is. Or that she would recognize them as one of her kind. I dread the day when she stumbles into the world of humans.

IT TAKES her another three years before she accepts that she is indeed a different kind of dragon. One devoid of scales, wings, and breath of fire. She is no less fierce for it. She lets her nails grow long to have claws like me. She grinds flowers and berries into clay, smearing the concoction along her face and arms to match my coloring. She bares her teeth and growls when angry. Her temper is as hot as the fire that flows from my mouth.

She wears the pelts of animals I have killed as her dinner. She still cannot bring herself to kill them, though she knows we rely on them for sustenance. Neither the wild nor the dragon she has grown to know could ever erase the purity of her soul. Her secret sweet loving nature only I am privileged to witness.

Her imagination has grown wild these days. She discovered the castle in the distance for the first time this morning. "What is that?" she asks, pointing to her true home.

"It's called a castle."

"Like the place in your stories?" I nod my head, turning back for the cave. She sprawls out on my back, her eyes studying the clouds above us. "Does a princess live there, like in the stories?"

The hope in her voice stills my heart. Do I tell her the truth? "I wouldn't know, Esme." Yes, I am a true coward. But she is still too young, I tell myself. It makes me feel a little better.

"Maybe we should check. She might need saving."

I sigh out and shake my head at her as if she has exasperated me. "She wouldn't want us to save her."

"Why not? We're plenty strong."

We stop at the mouth of the cave and I feel her slide off my back. She walks around to face me, her fists planted on her hips.

"And we're dragons. Humans fear dragons. Humans save other humans."

"Well, can't dragons save humans too?"

"If there is a dire need to," I say. She nods once at this, seeming pleased, and strolls into the cave. She makes me proud, and I find myself murmuring aloud, "Sometimes, we can even love them."

THE YEAR PASSED by in a blur, but Esme's curiosity only grew. I had ingrained in her the dangers humans could pose since she had come to me. Oh, but my stubborn little fool just can't help herself at this traveling party that passes near our mountain. They are not from these lands if they brave coming this close to my lair.

Esme has seen plenty horses in her eight years of life, but never the tamed ones. She watches them, fascination in her eyes as they pass by in a steady trot. She ducks down further at the voices of the men, and I am relieved she has heeded my warnings. She looks bored until the party stops, and a woman steps out of the coach.

The woman is dressed in fine clothes, her dress a dark scarlet. Her hair is pinned up, but she takes this moment to let it down. Esme touches her own hair, her fingers barely able to pass through the snarled ends. The woman laughs, and it sounds like a rain shower of small bells. I am also almost as enchanted by this woman as Esme seems to be.

The woman speaks to the men a moment longer before climbing back into the coach. They crowd together, passing some type of drink between them, before setting off once more. Esme stays hidden in the grass long after they have left. I notice her restlessness later that night, and the way her hand constantly strokes over her wild tangles.

THE TREE she once tried to fly from is now her quiet place, the place where she daydreams. She stares at the castle and imagines what lays behind those magnificent walls. If only she knew that she is of that castle, having been born behind those very walls. I haven't the heart to tell her the truth of what dwells there now. Knowledge of an enemy king who cut down her family would dash her fairy tale musings.

She demands to know more about humans, especially the ones we saw. "What is the one with the long fur called?"

I stall, not wanting to reveal the truth to her, but I am also her only teacher. I cannot lie. "That was a woman. A human female."

"I have long fur on my head."

I nod my head and watch her as she weaves flowers together in a sort of crown. If only she knew of the true crown that awaits her. "Because you are also a female."

Her fingers continue working the small stems, bending and twisting. Her eyebrows furrow together as she mulls over my words. "And she did not have scales." I let out a noncommittal sound of agreement. "Or wings."

"And?"

She looks up at me, her emeralds sparking with their realization. "She is just like me." The words cut through me. She has finally realized what she truly is. Will she learn to fear me now?

My next question weighs heavy on my tongue, but I must ask. "Do you think you're human too?" She smiles as she holds up her completed crown, and I lower my head to the ground. She places it on the tip of my ear and stands back to admire her handiwork.

"No, I think you were wrong. She is just another pitiful dragon, like me." The relief is overwhelming, and a small guilty part of me knows I should correct her. But perhaps she doesn't wish to be human. Her soul is wholly dragon. I nuzzle her cheek and close my eyes.

"No, Esme, you are truly one of a kind."

ESME VENTURED CLOSER to the castle as she neared her ninth year of life. She became bolder in her investigations. She still believes she is a dragon, but humans are her newest obsession. She studies them from afar, as she doesn't trust them yet. I hope she never trusts them.

SHE WAS PICKING berries the day they found her. The men shouted to one another, about the wildling they stumbled across. They asked her name. She answered honestly. Her greatest teacher forgot to teach her the value of a lie. It didn't take long for them to put the pieces together. *The lost princess,* they gasped. I wish I could say I was there to witness this, but I only found out through hushed rumors.

Her shrieking is what alerted me. My Esme never cried out in fear. My heart pounded, the fire in my chest raged, and I charged down the mountain. But they had her on horseback, galloping away, and if I attacked them, she would perish with them. I would have to bide my time.

THEY HAVE her placed in the tallest tower. I peek into her window, the moonlight aiding me in spotting her. Her skin is a creamy white, her hair smooth as it fans out against her pillow. She looks just like the princesses I told her about. She has found her rightful place.

I turn to leave her, knowing that despite the heartache it will cause me, this is what is best for her. But she somehow spots me in the darkness. I hear her sniffles and turn around. She leans out as far as she can to touch me, and I place my snout close to her hand, just as when we first met.

"They washed away my scales," she whimpers out.

"The smoothness suits you."

She holds her hands out and hangs her head. "They cut my claws."

"You won't need to fight here."

She looks back up at me, and fists a chunk of her hair. "They tamed my fur."

I can't help the chuckle that escapes me. My insistent little fool. "Then make it wild again."

Her hands fall in front of her, her fists clenched into tiny balls. "I look like the humans."

My heart stalls, then thunders in my ears. It is time. She must know the truth, and I'd rather her hear it from me. "That, my child, is because you are one." The tears that stream down her face are silent and slow. They glisten in the moonlight, leaving fresh paths along her cleaned cheeks.

"Did you steal me?" The fear in those words break my heart. Does she think I am evil? Have the humans already filled her head?

"I saved you."

She raises her knee, as if to climb out of the window. I back away, but it doesn't stop her. With both knees on the ledge, her hands grasping at the sides of her window, she pleads, "Then save me again. I want to go home." She will be the death of me.

"Esme, *this* is your home." I nuzzle her cheek before whipping away into the night.

She calls out to me in the darkness, but I don't turn back. As much as I want to tear off the top of that tower and scoop her up, I know I can't. It is like the old woman said. She very well may be the kingdom's last hope.

NINE YEARS HAVE PASSED. Nine long, lonely years. I tried to leave this place, to make a new home for myself. But what if, I ask myself, what if Esme comes back? No, this is home until the day she takes her last breath. I haven't seen her since our last goodbye at the castle. I wonder what she looks like now.

I've heard stories, stories of her beauty and her strength. I've heard grumblings of her stubborn nature and her refusal to stay indoors. I've heard the whispers, of her obsession with dragons and wildflowers. I often sit by her tree and stare at her castle. It doesn't sound like she has changed one bit, but there is nothing to indicate that she misses me. Has she forgotten me?

"Dragon!" I hear a female's voice bellow out, echoing against the walls of my cave. It sounds angry and fierce. No one has risked challenging me in a long time. What woman would dare come here? Unless...

A tall, lithe woman, clad in armor meets me in the middle of my cave. Her hair sways behind her like a thick inky waterfall as she marches closer to me. She takes in the interior, her eyes studying the walls and the markings Esme long ago carved in as a child. Eyes that flash with their emerald glint. *Esme.*

"Why have you come, dressed as a warrior?"

"I have come to kill you!" It comes out as a roar, much like mine when in battle.

"Is that so?" I am goading her, but I long to hear more of her voice.

"Yes. My Coronation Day is next week, and if I am to prove to be a reliable ruler, I must slay you." Her voice is nothing like the woman we saw on the road when she was merely eight. No soft tinkling sound for my little one. Her voice comes out in a raspy hard edge, commanding and strong.

It appears the kingdom wishes to rid itself of its resident dragon. I wonder, what threat I could possibly pose these days? I'd never attack the castle now that Esme resides there. Or perhaps they fear I'll come back for her. "Is that what they told you?"

"Yes."

I tap my claw on the floor, as if deep in thought, and smirk as her eyes study the movement. I wonder if she misses her own claws, or even remembers them. "Wouldn't your blood alone prove you a reliable ruler?"

She huffs out, and I imagine real smoke would come out if she were as dragon as she once believed herself to be. She thrusts her sword in my face, her eyes glaring up into mine. I rest my chin on the ground and huff back, letting the warm steam wash over her.

Her eyes narrow, and her head tilts slightly. "Tell me, dragon, do I know you?" My heart sinks as her question confirms my worst fears. She doesn't remember. Do I look that different? She hasn't changed. Still so full of questions.

"Do you?"

"I've dreamt of you. I made you flower crowns and rode your back. I curled up to sleep within your wings and kissed your scales."

I close my eyes, secretly delighting in the memories. Those puny humans couldn't taint her dragon soul, though I imagined they tried. "Maybe you did know me, once upon a time." I open my eyes and watch her take in my lair with renewed wonder.

"Why do I feel such hatred for you? I look at you and feel betrayed." Her eyes glimmer up at me, more beautiful than my memories served.

I nod my head, remembering the way I abandoned her. Of

course, she would hate me. "If you hate me, then you should kill me."

She takes a shuddering breath, the tip of her sword pressing in between my eyes. Her bottom lip trembles, and she stills it with her teeth. "I don't," she whispers out, dropping her sword. "Not really. Deep inside, I feel we are one and the same."

My heart swells. She is still mine, even after all these years. My precious little fool.

"What bothers you?" I ask as a whimper escapes her.

She hugs herself and shakes her head, her eyes meeting mine. "I've only wanted to be fearsome, and I can't even slay the mighty dragon to prove my worth."

I straighten and bow my head in reverence. "You are the most fearsome being that has ever entered this cave." And I mean it. Even when she was a wriggling little thing, all swaddled up in blood stained cloth, she scared me.

She sighs and leans on her sword. "I wish I didn't have to kill you."

"Do you want to rule the kingdom?"

She shakes her head in denial, not even giving it a second thought.

I nod my head and lift her chin with my claw. "Tell me, Esme, what it is you truly desire."

She doesn't pull away. She doesn't fear me at all, though I could slice her in half if I chose to. Instead, she huffs out in an indignant way and juts out her chin. "You'll think I'm silly."

"I promise not to laugh."

She closes her own eyes now and a sad smile barely lifts the corners of her lips. "I wish to fly. Then I could fly away from here and be free."

I rumble out my approval and flatten myself to the ground.

"Climb on, my little dragon, and let me be your wings."

DOUBLE HELIX

LUCIA IGLESIAS

I stepped into the bath. The stone floor sloped, a gentle helix, spiraling me into the steaming pool. Water beaded the cavern walls, as if the entire bathing cave were strung with pearls. Stepping through veils of steam, I spiraled deeper into the pool.

At the center, I was waist-deep. As water seeped into my pelt, I felt like a lodestone, water drawn to me like iron filings, turning my fur black and dragging at my edges. Sinking in, I found the sloping path with my fingertips and sat on its rim, water right up to my chin. Steam hung above the pool in gossamer sheets, so thick I could only see one pool beyond mine.

I closed my eyes and rested my head on the slick stone, letting the water creep between the hairs on the back of my neck. The smell of sulfur was thick in my throat, the smell of silver and geysers and fire in the belly of the earth.

I was hungry. I had been hungry for six days. Nothing made it go away. Mushroom steaks, lichen cakes, chicory coffee by the potful, even a fine filet of chanterelle. There wasn't a delicacy in the entire cave city that would still my stomach. I kept catching myself daydreaming about his fingers.

GRETTIR HAS STARFISH FINGERS. I once told him so when we were out tickling amethyst anemones in the tidepools of the subterranean sea. He didn't like it, but it's true. He has heavy hands, fingers long and tapered, golden skin that's always dry. Hairless. When I take his hands in mine, he flinches, tickled by the thick fur bristling round my fingerpads.

Cunning starfish fingers. Out at the tidepools, I used to collect specimens for him to sketch: a bucket brimming with ivory barnacles, indolent snails, indigo mussels, prickly limpets, spindly sea stars, and anemones balled up like angry fists. In his sketches: every spine and armored shell realized in hard charcoal. Every line, every shadow, every highlight alive. I have never seen Grettir throw away a sketch. He doesn't throw away so much as a line. Every stroke is heavy with intention.

To DISTRACT MYSELF, I dipped my face in the quicksilver water, watching the ripples melt lazily away as I shook sparklets from my eyelashes. Underwater, I ran my fingers down my arms, combing out the fur with my fingernails. Then I did my legs, my belly, my back. It felt good to get my fingers in my fur, combing through the knots. Sometimes it feels like I'm a sack of skin stitched too tight to my bones. Hot water and a good combing can loosen the seams.

I rubbed my back against the stone for a good scratch and felt my fur catch. When I cursed and wrenched away, I felt several hairs ripping from my skin. With my fingers, I traced back over the place and found a spine rippling the smooth stone. A fossil. A helix of lithified bone. Ammonite.

ALL HE'S BEEN SKETCHING LATELY: SPIRALING shells locked in stone. Not uncommon in the cave city—most families have a fossil or two protruding from the stone walls of their parlors. Often framed, pressed under a pane, long-dead cephalopods in glass coffins. But Grettir likes the undomesticated specimens: ammonite on alley walls, or in the southern subcaverns still untouched by urban sprawl.

I watch his cunning fingers speak the specimens to life in charcoal and light. A language only he speaks—language of lines, loops, ellipses, sickle moons, sweet ratios—a symphony in black and white.

He gives his nub of charcoal to me so he can brush his hands clean and hold the picture up to the light. He angles it so the rays skating down a nearby sky-shaft skim softly over the page. It's perfect. The ammonite on the page: alive in light and shadow. The ammonite on the wall: dead. Entombed in echoing stone. He holds the drawing out to me, fingers fanning off the page until he holds it between pinky and thumb.

"For you," he says, his voice settling like dust on the cavern hush.

~

I PUSHED off the wall and stood up. Fed by springs boiling up through the earth's veins, the pools never cooled, and I could already feel a film of sweat hot on my forehead. My stomach growled.

Angrily, I shook the water from my pelt, spinning so the spray pinwheeled out around me. I clamped my hands over my belly, crushing it silent, even as static electricity spooked the hairs around my fingerpads. The fur on my stomach stood up, dark spindles shivering in the steam.

This six-day-old hunger.

~

"FOR YOU," he says again, holding out the picture to me. "You've had a hard week."

I look down at my left hand, the half-healed crescent where my sister bit down to the bone. Six days tender. Red ridges wrinkling my fur. It's hard looking after her, half-grown but all wild, nothing like I was at that age. As if the bear in our blood weren't thinned with human, as if our forebear bore *her*, not our six-generations-great grandmother.

My sister, with her white pelt and our father's blue-black eyes. All I want is to gather her up in my arms and tell her sister-secrets. But whenever I try, she shakes me off and paces the edges of the parlor. She hasn't been allowed out since the biting.

"Trade you," Grettir says, nodding at the nub of charcoal sticking out of my right hand. He holds the drawing out so that they almost touch, the charcoal and his index finger. That cunning finger, long and tapered, skin thin and golden, blue veins pale and fine as candyfloss beneath the surface.

I bow my head over our hands—his extended finger, the charcoal stick, thick and crisp—as if for a kiss.

I can't help myself.

I take a bite.

THE BONE POET AND GOD

MATT DOVEY

Ursula lifted her snout to look at the mountain. The meadowed foothills she stood in were dotted with poppy and primrose and cranesbill and cowslip, an explosion of color and scent in the late spring sun, the long grass tickling her paws and her hind legs; above that the forested slopes, birch and rowan and willow and alder rising into needle-pines and gray firs; above that the snowline, ice and rock and brutal winds.

And above that, at the top, God; and with God, the answer Ursula had traveled so far for: *what kind of bear am I meant to be?* She shouldered her bonesack and walked on.

THERE WAS a shuffling sound among the bracken, small but definite. Ursula hesitated, a dry branch held in her paws, her campfire half-built. Ambush wasn't unheard of—so many bears sought God on the mountain that bonethieves couldn't resist the chances to steal—but it had not been so large a sound, and she couldn't smell another bear beneath the pine scent. It was something smaller, lurking in the dim light of the forest floor, behind the massive rough-barked firs that filled the slope.

"Hello?" she ventured, still holding motionless. "It's quite all right. I'm building a fire, if you'd like to join me."

A badger stepped out from the ferns, his snout twitching and cautious, a stout stick held warily in his paws. He eyed Ursula for a moment, weighing up the situation, and she gestured ever so gently to the fire she was building, trying to come across as safe, as friendly. As likeable.

He straightened and walked forward. He kept the stick before him, but Ursula understood. Bears could be dangerous.

Two more badgers followed him, one much smaller—"Oh, you're a family!" said Ursula. "I'll make a seat for you!"

She stood, turned, dashed back, dropping to four paws in her enthusiasm. She ran to where she'd seen a fallen log not twenty yards away by the river and hauled it back, her claws dug into its softened bark, dragging it and dropping it by the fire pit with a thud. She grinned at the family, proud of her resourcefulness—

The badgers cowered, the two behind the father with the stick, who tried to meet her eyes but couldn't help glancing away for places to burrow and hide.

Ursula lowered herself slowly to sit. She made a point of picking up smaller twigs to lay on the fire, the least threatening pieces she could find. "Sorry," she said quietly. "I forget how I can come across. Please. Sit down." She concentrated on building the fire, determinedly not looking at the badgers, not wanting to startle them, trying not to let their fear hurt her nor to berate herself for getting carried away and upsetting others. For letting her shyness get to her: for overcompensating for it.

If only she knew who she was, instead of pretending so poorly.

"Thank you," said Father Badger from the log, and Ursula smiled at him, keeping her teeth covered. "Forgive us our caution. We... have never met a bear before."

"I'm Ursula," she said.

"My name is Patrick," said Father Badger, "and this is my husband, Willem, and our new daughter Ann."

"And how old are you, Ann?" Another careful smile, friendly not fearsome, benevolent not bearlike.

Ann shuffled a little and squirmed in closer to Willem, who put an arm around her.

"She is a little shy," said Willem. "We only met her an hour ago."

"She's why we came up the mountain," said Patrick, smiling at his daughter. "Willem and I came to ask God for a blessing, and we found Ann burrowed alone beneath a root."

"God showed you to her?" said Ursula eagerly, forgetting her calm façade in her excitement. "Is she near?"

"We never saw God," said Willem, "and now we have no need. God has delivered us our gift already."

"Oh," said Ursula. "I mean, I'm happy for you! I really am. I just..."

"You hoped she would be near?" finished Willem.

Ursula shrugged, not trusting herself to speak. She put the

last branch on the fire and hooked a claw around the strap of her bonesack, bones rattling inside the plain leather.

She felt, rather than saw, the badgers tense.

"You're a bonethief," said Patrick, voice flat and accusatory.

"We were warned of your kind on the mountainside," said Willem, pulling Ann in close.

"They're not my kind," said Ursula carefully. "I don't do what they do."

"You carry the bones," said Patrick. His paw lay on the stout stick, though if she truly were a bonethief it'd do him no use. She admired him that bravery, that certainty in his actions.

"Not all bears that carry bones are bonethieves," said Ursula. "There is so much more that can be done. Please. Let me show you."

She reached into the bag and started pulling bones out, laying them on the floor, runes up. She spoke as she did, her voice low and even, trying to defuse the situation she had accidentally escalated again. "Every bone is from a family member. They've all passed down to me, bit by bit. This one here was Aunt Maud's, this one Uncle Arthur's, that there is my Great-Grandma's right arm. Every bear carries four runes on their body—well, usually, by the end... anyway—four runes carved into their bones. One is carved on the left thigh bone at birth by one parent, another on the right thigh by the other when they consider their child has come of age."

"How?" asked Willem, still cautious, but curious too.

"Bear claws are sharp," Ursula said. "I would show you with mine, but I don't want to scare Ann." She tried a smile again, only a small one, tentative, but Ann responded in kind. "My parents cut through my flesh to carve their chosen rune on my bones. Their words hold me up everywhere I go, even this far from them. My father gave me HOME at birth and my mother gave me WATER. It helps me miss them less, as if they're with me wherever I am."

The bones were all laid out now, and Ursula began to choose from them. SUN, from Great-Great-Uncle Morris. WIND to cross it: Grandma Oak's breastbone.

"The third," she continued, "is given to us by God, shaped on our breastbone from the very moment of our conception. None of us ever know our breastbone rune. It's only known when we pass our bones to our family." She began to lay the bones before the fire pit. SLEEP, the next.

"And the fourth?" asked Patrick.

Ursula paused. She kept her voice flat when she answered, trying not to let any emotion into her answer. "The fourth we carve ourselves, on our right arm." She chose WAKE from the pile, and put it in place:

A hot gust of air blew towards the campfire and it flared into life, awakening to a satisfying crackle. A gentle, sloopy warmth washed over Ursula, and she smiled to herself in satisfaction, then began putting bones back into the sack.

"I'm a bone poet," she said. "The bonethieves only ever work towards violence and supremacy. All the bones they steal are only to help them steal more bones. They never think of all the better ways bones can be used."

"How do you know what to choose?" asked Ann. Willem looked down at her in surprise.

"Well, the contraries must share something to bind the square together but have a tension that will give it power, and the neighbors should resonate in sound or form to amplify it, and the whole has to work to the purpose. I suppose I know what to choose because I know my bones well, what I've inherited and what might work."

"No," said Ann. "How do you choose what you carve on your own arm?"

"Oh." Ursula picked a branch up, nudged at the fire with it, re-arranged the piled sticks to get them burning better. She mostly only knocked it over. "That's... that's what I want to ask God about."

"Why?"

Ursula stared into the fire. How to express it? How to encapsulate the paralysis of choice, the fear of choosing wrong, the strange position of not knowing yourself?

"There is power in four," she said, still staring. "Four bones combine into a poem of purpose. All of them interact and reinforce each other. I have to choose my own fourth rune carefully so that my purpose as a bear is strong. But how can I choose the fourth when only God knows what my third is?"

"So you go to ask," said Willem.

Ursula nodded, feeling small, shrunken by her uncertainty, so unbearlike. "Choosing your own rune is... is the act of choosing who you want to be. It's the moment of knowing yourself and defining yourself. Of finding your place in the world. But I don't know who I am yet. Other bears just seem to know, but me... I try to be what I think other people need me to be, but it feels like everyone wants me to be something different, and every time I think I know which rune I should choose something changes my mind."

"It is admirable that you worry so much about others," said

Willem. "Perhaps you should worry more about yourself, though. It sounds like this should be about you, not about the world."

She prodded at the fire again. It felt—strange, to vocalize what had been churning and building in her head for so long. Stranger yet to be telling it to a badger cub. She looked up to smile at Ann, not a calming smile, but a real smile, a vulnerable smile, a—

Patrick had raised his stick, and was looking past Ursula. She turned, frowning, staring into the gloom of dusk that swam through the trees. There wasn't—no, a glint—eyes reflecting flame—then a snarl, and Ursula's fur bristled in alarm, and a sudden gust of icy wind extinguished the fire and knocked the badgers backwards.

Bone magic.

Bonethief.

"Run!" shouted Ursula to the badgers. She scooped up her bonesack and went to run too, but Ann was so small, and ran so slowly, too slowly, and Ursula realized the badgers would never escape.

She dropped her bonesack and began digging through it for bones. She only had to slow the bonethief enough for Patrick and Willem to get Ann underground, then she could run too. She couldn't risk her bones. The bonethief ran forward on all fours, bones held in his jaws: he was a huge grizzly, bigger than Ursula, his fur matted with green-brown moss and sticky sap.

He pulled up at the sight of her bonesack—not in fear, she didn't think, but in avarice.

"So," he growled, low and fearsome, "you've been thieving round here for some time."

Ursula drew herself up tall, her fur raised, trying to make herself seem confident and sure. "I have not. I'm no bonethief."

"Quite the sack of bones you've got there for a bear traveling alone. Or are those little badgers your companions, and not just a snack you're luring in?"

Ursula risked a glance back at them—Ann had stopped to watch, and was refusing to be pulled away—and it hurt her to worry they might believe him for even a moment. Surely they already knew her better! But she had to seem strong and bear-like now: she couldn't show any concern for smaller creatures in front of this other bear.

She lifted her snout. "My family has entrusted them to me and my skill. I am a bone poet." She said this with as much pride as she could in the hopes it would impress the bonethief, forge a connection between them and allow her to talk herself out of this without any conflict.

But it did not. He laughed, a deep roar, a bellow of mirth that shook needles loose from the pines. "A poet? What fresh scat is this?"

His mockery stung, but not just because she'd failed to impress him. No, it stung because she *was* proud to be a bone poet, she realized. She was proud of the things she could do. She was proud of the connections she could make between bones.

She was proud of the way Ann had looked at her as she explained. She *was* better than this thief.

"I'm more deserving of these bones than you'll ever be." Her voice now was angry, not by choice, not to elicit a response from him, but because she *meant* it.

The thief grinned back at her, exposing his fangs. "Doesn't matter if you deserve them. Only matters if you're strong enough to keep them from me." His paws moved to his bones, and he began laying out his square.

Not enough time to think, only to react. Ursula grabbed bones from her sack almost without thought, going by touch and instinct, and laid them out in a square:

RISE ROOT &EARTH FALL

The soil beneath the bonethief fell away like melting snow and the exposed tree roots started to twist and writhe, a tangle of wood squirming with life. The bear stumbled and fell into the trap, snarling, swiping at the roots as his back legs sunk into the soft ground.

Willem was scrabbling at the earth, burrowing, as Patrick stood before Ann with his stick held out. It'd do no more than scratch the throat of the bonethief as he swallowed. His bravery brought her heart to her throat.

The bonethief roared. "Stupid sow! I'll take all your bones! I'll rip yours from your flesh!" He grasped at the roots, hauling himself out of the loose mud.

Ursula rifled through her bones again. She had to do something else to slow him down, so she could—

No. She had to do something to stop him. If he didn't get her bones, he'd chase someone else's. He'd eat other small mammals he came across, hurt other travelers. But she was a bone poet, and she could outthink him. She could stop him here.

The bonethief was free of the earth now, arranging his small clutch of stolen bones to send another blast of icy wind; she could see the runes from here, WIND and WILD and

STRONG and ICE. She chose her bones with more care, though no less speed:

Her square burst with light, and even knowing it was coming it was all Ursula could do to shield her eyes, positioning herself to protect the badgers. The bonethief was less prepared—staring greedily at Ursula, at her bonesack—and the full flash of light blinded him. He yelped in agony, in surprise, as the sight was burned from his eyes. If she had done enough he would no longer be able to read the runes on bones. She doubted he could recognize them by touch.

But he, too, had finished his square: and he was closer to her this time, and the blast of wind gusted hard. With her paws raised to shield her eyes from her own blast, Ursula was unbalanced, and she was knocked backwards, down the slope, all her bones scattering in the chill wind, and she rolled and fell towards the river and into the river and knocked her head and—

ICY WATER SPLASHED at Ursula's snout. Slapped at it, even. She stirred, groggily, and opened her eyes to a salmon flopping on her face. She swiped at it unthinkingly, knocking it away, then groaned as she realized how hungry she was.

With an effort, she hauled herself from the river and shook the water from her fur. In the dim light of dusk it was difficult to tell how exactly far she had fallen down the mountain, but the ground around her sloped only gently, covered in tall grass and meadow flowers closed for the night.

She was as far from God as she had ever been, and she no longer had her bones. She no longer had her friends—oh, she hoped Patrick and Willem and Ann had gotten away! Surely they were small enough and quick enough to avoid a blinded bear?—and she was not sure she had hope, either. It had taken days to ascend the mountain before, when she had her bones to intuit the way and catch leaping salmon and all the other little helps her poems gave her. Could she do it again now? What if another bonethief found her? Even without her bonesack to steal, she could be killed for her own bones.

But what else? Go home, and never know who she was? Never know who she should be? Could be?

Ursula pulled herself to her paws, cold muscles rasping, and dragged herself up the slope.

Walking on all fours in her exhaustion, her head bowed, the sun long set, Ursula trudged through the forest, stumbling wearily into alders and birches, knocking some over with a creaking, snapping shock of sound, loud in the silence of the night, stirring birds from their sleep in a panic. She fell into an atavistic trance: cold, hungry, determined, focused only on the ascent, forgetting even why she climbed, lost wholly in her drive to get higher, higher, higher.

So it was that she became aware of the light only slowly.

The color of it was the first thing she noticed. It was too blue for dawn. As she lifted her head to look closer, she saw the strangeness of the shadows—flickering, oddly angled, moving with each tired step like a broken branch swaying in the wind.

And she looked up at last, and saw a sleek black bear walking beside her, smaller, lither, and glowing gently.

"Hello Ursula," said God. "Would you like something to eat?" God gestured towards a clearing, where three salmon hung by a small, crackling fire that could not have been there a moment before. Had the clearing even been there?

Ursula lumbered forward and fell onto her haunches by the fire, snatching one of the salmon with a swipe and chewing it in silence, still lost in her animal exhaustion. God busied herself with the trees as Ursula ate, shaping branches with a touch and humming softly as she did, new leaves sprouting where her claws danced.

"Have I—" said Ursula, once she had eaten, warmed, returned to herself—"have I walked so long I am at the top?" She looked about at the trees, but they were still broad-leafed, of the low slopes.

God smiled up at a rowan; she reinvigorated one final branch with an upwards stroke, stretching on her hind legs, then sat down before Ursula. She exuded—*contentment.*

"No," she said, her voice high and clear like birdsong at dawn. "I am rarely at the top. It's so desolate up there, beautiful as it is. The point of the mountain is only to see how determined pilgrims are. Patrick and Willem could never have ascended above the snowline, but they climbed so far on such small legs. If they had that devotion in them, if they were so driven by love, then Ann could do no better than their care."

Ursula's throat tightened in fear for the badgers. "Did they —are they—"

"Yes," said God, "they are fine. You did enough. Thank you."

Tension flooded out of Ursula like meltwater. The thought had weighed heavy, but—but they were well. She hoped they would be happy together.

"I believe, by the way," said God, "that these are yours." She reached behind where she was sat—where there had been nothing but grass and fallen twigs a moment before—and produced Ursula's bonesack, clearly full.

Ursula lurched forward with a gasp, snatching the bag quite before she could comprehend the rudeness of what she had done, and to whom she had done it.

"There are," said God, "a few more bones in there than before. You will be a better keeper for them, I think."

Ursula's breath caught in a sudden clench of nervousness, and she lowered the bag. So long spent climbing the slope, anticipating this moment, and now she couldn't get her words in order. There was so much to say, such an entwined web of emotion and expectation and duty and hope and thought and fear that she couldn't possibly order it anymore, couldn't untangle it to find the starting thread, couldn't do more than hold the whole concept of what she needed in her head at once, complete and connected and indivisible.

But she had come all this way, and perhaps if she just started. "About bones—"

"I know," said God. "Of course I know." And she smiled again, and stood up and walked over and hugged Ursula tight. Her glow expanded to surround them both, and the contentment too.

She spoke in Ursula's ear. "The rune on your breastbone doesn't matter. You can complete your own poem without knowing. You don't need to know who you are to choose who you want to be. You don't need to let other people's choices in your past define your future. It doesn't matter what I wrote when I made you in the swirling potential of the Before, when the path to your existence and that rune was laid in the What Nexts—it only matters what you feel now."

"But I need to finish the poem of my bones! If I don't choose the right rune to complete the four, to complement the three I've got, my purpose won't be as strong as it could be!"

"Ursula, you are not a poem, you are a bear," God admonished. "You do not have to be a purpose—you are the purpose. You are *who* you are, not what you can offer."

God released Ursula, held her shoulders in her paws, smiled at her through brimming tears and a face filled with pride. "The words you have on your bones already were only meant to get you this far, when you could decide for yourself whom you wanted to be."

Ursula choked back a sob, but the dam burst anyway, and she cried into God's shoulder. With relief, with possibility. With acceptance.

God held her there a long while, as the sun rose and the earth warmed and the flowers opened to the sky.

"What do you think you will choose, then?" asked God. "I will help carve it, as an honor to you, and as thanks for saving the badgers."

Ursula looked at her bonesack, and thought of all the poems waiting in there, all the combinations and implications and things that could be. And now, with the new bones, there were so many more possibilities, so much still to see and learn. So much still unknown.

"I don't know," said Ursula. "I don't know at all, yet."

And for the first time, that answer gave her contentment.

THE HEDGEHOG AND THE PINE CONE

GWYNNE GARFINKLE

This is the story of Purple and Green, two hedgehogs who were the best of friends. They rolled and played on the forest floor. The hedgehogs were spiny and guarded, but they knew how to reach each other. They feasted on berries and mushrooms, bright frogs and luminous snails, while they told each other the funniest and saddest and strangest stories they could think of. Some were stories they'd read in books, while others were anecdotes they'd heard from other hedgehogs or happenings from their own lives. Even calamities that had befallen them became fodder for their stories, offered up for each other's enjoyment.

Then one morning, Purple found that Green had turned into a pine cone, armored and inanimate. Purple butted her head against Green, but instead of giggling or waddling in a circle or poking Purple with her snout, she wobbled and grew still once more. "Green, please speak to me," Purple implored. "How did this happen? Did you will it so, or was it done to you? Are you under a spell?" Green didn't reply. Purple couldn't tell if Green had a heartbeat anymore, or a heart.

Purple sat with Green for a long time, waiting for the pine cone to come back to life. She told Green funny stories, but the pine cone didn't laugh. She brought Green mushrooms and berries and the very best snails she could find and laid them where her feet used to be, but the pine cone made no move to eat them. Green's silence and stillness became unbearable. Purple pushed Green hard with her paws and cried, "What is the matter with you?" Green wobbled, then grew motionless. Purple let out a snarl that turned into a sob.

At last Purple turned to walk away, but she turned back again and again, hoping Green would make some move to stop her. The pine cone didn't seem to care. Green made no sign that she even noticed as Purple trudged away.

Purple wandered disconsolate through the forest, the vibrant green all around only reminding the hedgehog of her lost and silent friend. Birds chittered and sang arpeggios to each other. She was silent and alone, her eyes heavy with tears. Then an owl swooped down and tried to catch her in its talons, and Purple roused herself from her sorrow and ran as fast as she could. She crouched shivering and miserable under a thorny shrub until the owl winged away, hooting imperiously.

The hedgehog worried that the owl might find Green, but she wasn't near enough to warn her. Purple hoped that at least as a pine cone, Green would be safe from the owl's predations.

The hedgehog crawled out from beneath the shrub and looked around. She had reached an unfamiliar part of the forest. Instead of leaves and fruit, the trees all sprouted books. Some of the trees, especially the smaller, younger ones, were sparsely leaved with volumes. The more massive trees were loaded with them.

Many books had fallen onto the ground. Beneath the larger trees, the forest floor was carpeted with volumes. Purple glanced at their covers as she walked over the books. Morocco leather bindings mingled with lurid paperback covers. She idly riffled the pages of one book after another. Some books appeared pristine, while others seemed to have been well-thumbed, even underlined and annotated. She wasn't sure if these had been read on the ground or if intrepid readers had climbed trees to peruse them. She thought some of the books might contain stories that Green would enjoy, and then she remembered her loss afresh and began to cry. Her tears fell onto the book covers, and she dried them with her paws the best she could.

One book drew Purple's attention. It was a paperback with green leaves and purple flowers on the cover. The hedgehog nosed it open. There were no dog-eared pages, no underlines or annotations. Purple climbed inside and pulled the pages shut. She wandered the forest of letters, black trees against an off-white sky. The words sheltered the hedgehog against the pine cone's silence. Purple called Green's name, and it echoed off the page.

The book held the hedgehog in its paper embrace, enveloped her in its clean and slightly musty smell. It rocked her to sleep. Stories sidled through her dreams, and she thought Green might be there too, flitting among the tales. First there was the story of a mother's deep, winter-causing grief when her daughter was stolen away to the underworld; when the daughter returned, her mother's rejoicings brought spring to the land. Next was the story of a lover transformed into a snake, then a fire, then a lion—biting and singeing his beloved as she held on—until at last, due to her determination, he turned back into himself, and not a wordless, eyeless tree.

Purple already knew these two stories, but the third was new to her. It was the tale of an inveterate reader who died before he could read the last chapters of a gripping novel and who spent his afterlife amid the book's characters and situations, trying to figure out how it ended. He tried out tragic endings and happy ones, endings improbable and rote, until at last he happened upon the perfect ending, both unexpected and inevitable, and he was able to rest satisfied.

When Purple woke, she wandered deeper into the maze of words, towards the book's heart, her own heart, the world's heart. Green was part of that, whether the pine cone knew it or not. Purple became convinced that Green did still have a heart, whether or not she had a heartbeat. The book-forest was dotted with the small shrubs of *the* and *and* and *but*, the great towering trees of *circumstance* and *loyalty*, the bright flame-like flowers of *grief* and *surprise*. The words were beacons. The words were companions. The words were heartbeats, urging Purple on.

She kept thinking about the final story in her dream. She thought that Green would like that story, about the reader trying to find the ending to the book. *I believe that Green is still alive*, Purple thought. *Even if she is silent and still, we are still alive, and our story may continue if I don't give up.*

At last the hedgehog came to a clearing and saw Green. Was she still a pine cone? Purple moved closer. Green stood alone in the empty space between one chapter and the next. Her spines —was Purple imagining?—no, it was true, her spines quivered ever so slightly. Green was a hedgehog again! She looked up at Purple. Something about Green's eyes made Purple hang back, but all of Purple's words rushed forth to say themselves. She told Green about the owl, and the forest of books, and the three stories. "But nothing seems real unless I can tell you about it," Purple said. "Green, can you hear me? Are you yourself again?"

For a long moment she feared it was all for naught. Then Green waddled closer to her. "Yes, Purple, I can hear you," she said, "and I am myself again, my friend." She told Purple the story of her imprisonment in the form of a pine cone, able to hear but not reply, able to see her friend and the forest around her, but unable to be a part of any of it. She said she had turned into a pine cone twice in the past, before they became friends.

"Why didn't you tell me?" Purple asked.

"It was the one story I could never bring myself to tell you," Green said. "I hoped it would never happen again. When it did, I heard you trying to reach me. I wanted to tell you not to go, but I couldn't. It was a kind of death in life. Finally the spell ended, and I looked everywhere for you. I feared that you had given up on me and gone so far away that I would never find you."

"I would never do that," Purple said, reproaching herself for running from Green when her friend had needed her most.

"At last I came to the forest of books," Green said. "I found this paperback and climbed inside. I got lost amid the shrubs of *the* and *and* and *but*, the great towering trees of *circumstance* and *loyalty*, and the bright flame-like flowers of *grief* and *surprise*. Finally I came to this empty space between chapters to rest, and you found me."

Purple wept for joy. Her happiness was so intense, she felt it could bring spring to the land. Together the hedgehogs made their way out of the book and found their way home. After that, they frequently visited the forest of books, where they met other readers who ventured there. Purple and Green combed through many volumes on the forest floor in search of the most beautiful stories to share with one another. And when, in the course of time, Green became a pine cone again, Purple stayed by her side and told her stories as she waited for her friend to return to her once more.

AS IF WAITING

A. KATHERINE BLACK

The fur on Aainah's legs shifted as Jwartan's tail wrapped around her ankles, seeking to comfort, or maybe to be comforted. She reached for his hand, unable to pull her gaze from the enormous serpent stretched across the valley below, at the creature that could not be and yet was, and she realized she should be filled with dread. But it was something else entirely that pressed against her ribs and somersaulted under her skin. It was exhilaration.

Large as half the village, the serpent oracle was still as stone, impossibly dark. Dark as all the tales told, rejecting the light of all four moons in the sky, as if this was something one could easily do.

It wasn't until she and Jwartan broke through the treeline at the crest of the hill and gazed upon the serpent oracle that Aainah realized she'd never believed it was real. She'd expected nothing but a gathering of boulders, maybe an odd line of fallen trees. Because it had to be nothing, didn't it? Nothing but a tale exaggerated to impossibility, like so many other myths spun by the elders to keep young ones in line. How could such a thing be true?

Just as no Onaphi could live at the river's bottom, gripping the fins of sharp-toothed beasts and riding the undercurrents to far away oceans, just as no Onaphi could stretch and weave their fur into wings and take to the sky to battle the fiercest of predator birds, surely no Onaphi could step into the body of an enormous serpent and emerge from its eye with a wisdom so rich it could cleanse the most wretched of souls. Who could really believe such a thing, especially, as her mother had said, when no one alive had even seen the serpent with their own eyes? Now facing the vast, motionless creature below, Aainah realized she'd expected, hoped, the journey alone would serve as her healing agent, would fix the wrongness that held fast and stubborn to the dark corners of her mind.

Aromas of unfamiliar territory floated up the hill. Odd grasses, dirt too metallic, unknown diurnal creatures hiding with hoards of wilting fruits. Scents wafted into her nostrils from the right and from the left, leaving a gaping hole in front of them. An odorless void hung in the direction of the serpent oracle, as if her nostrils suddenly clogged with the mucus of sickness whenever she gazed its way.

Craning her ears forward, Aainah heard not even a tiny

rustle. Not the slightest sigh of movement ahead. The entire clearing appeared as immobile as its giant inhabitant, as if holding its breath. As if waiting, for her.

If they ran toward it, right then, they might reach the oracle before daylight hit. Before the birds began hunting. There might have been time enough.

Jwartan gripped her shoulders. Shaking her gaze away from the serpent oracle, he asked that she give them one more day together. A final day. One last moment of now, before whatever was to be came to be. Aainah nestled her face in the crook of his neck. It was her favorite place in the world. She breathed in the dust of their long journey that clung now to his pelt. Of course, she said. She wouldn't have it any other way.

What she didn't say, despite the silent urging she felt from him, and from the village now many nights' journey away, even from the impatient rustle of the trees overhead, she didn't say she was sorry. Sorry for this exhausting journey, sorry for this budding excitement at witnessing the oracle before them. Sorry for being something other than what he wanted her to be. What everyone needed her to be.

Instead she slipped her arms around him and synced her breaths with his heartbeat, holding him close as she looked over his shoulder and through the trees at the Third Moon glistening above. The Third was her favorite for the same reason it was disliked by everyone else. It was the only moon whose face could not be seen, whose face was turned out, away from their world. Toward the stars.

As a young one, Aainah would ask her mother the same question every day before their sleep. What did the Third Moon see? What was it watching? Each time her mother swept the question aside with a small but firm flick of her tail, telling Aainah the Third watched nothing at all, because it had no face. How do you know, Aainah would ask. Because there is nothing else to see, her mother always said. There is nothing outside the villages and the waters, the mountains and the forests. If the third moon indeed had a face, her mother always said, it would be watching them. Aainah had stopped asking such questions around the same time she decided that there was more to life than her mother knew. Or than her mother wanted to know.

Curled together under a meager leaf shelter at the top of the hill, Aainah and Jwartan's throats rumbled in harmony as they moved in hungry rhythm, until sleep insisted on taking its turn. They woke at dusk, entangled, their dreams slipping away as the suns slipped from the sky. He whispered to her then, of the future they must have. Of the future they deserved.

She stroked his whiskers but held back the words dangling on her tongue. She didn't tell him that he was her only moonlight, the only beautiful thing in an otherwise bleak existence. Didn't try to explain the racing heart that screamed as she woke, screamed at the thought of doing the same work, night after night, of listening to the same stories and seeing the same faces, until every night crept agonizingly on toward a dull and hopeless forever. Her future in the village frightened Aainah to no end, more than the prospect of the oracle serpent devouring her alive, and she knew Jwartan would turn his ears against such a truth.

The final steps of their journey together took longer than expected. They arrived at the serpent's tail just as the first sun peeked over the horizon, spreading an uncomfortable warmth across Aainah's fur as her eyes darted toward the sky, sure there were as many predator birds in this valley as in any other.

Engulfed in the shadow of the serpent's tail, a tail that stretched higher than three of Aainah, she cursed the stories again. They never mentioned how to wake this oracle. Tales of the few who made the journey spent most of their words explaining the restlessness gnawing in the Onaphi's gut, detailing how they didn't fit in, how they couldn't fit in with their tribe. How they hid in their huts all night or paced the edges of the village relentlessly. Their tails constantly twitched, even during sleep, and no task offered sufficient reward, no company calmed their minds. These restless ones left the village long ago to journey to the serpent oracle, to beg for relief from the wrongness that infected their thoughts. Some emerged from the eye of the serpent and returned to the village, returned to life a satisfied, changed Onaphi. Others emerged only to abandon the village in favor of solitude in the forests. And there were those hopeless few who never emerged.

Gaining entry to the belly of this oracle might be a test, a trial. Aainah consciously suppressed the anxious tic in her tail, wondering if Jwartan was watching. She didn't turn to look. Instead she kept her ears craned on the puzzle of the oracle, refusing to add fuel to Jwartan's hope about her, about them.

The serpent's lack of motion, its lack of breath, was unsettling. Like the river monsters who lie in wait, still and deep under the surface of a stream, anxious to swallow whatever poor creature wandered too close. Feeling too much like one of those poor creatures, but not knowing what else to do, Aainah reached out and scraped a claw across the serpent's solid body. Her sharp touch made no sound, left no mark. Pressing a full hand to the serpent's side, Aainah felt an absence of cold, and an absence of warmth. It was like touching emptiness in solid form.

Sharp pain pierced a finger. Hissing, she jumped back, but could find no blemish on her hand, no spot tender to the touch. Still, something had bitten. Or stung.

She turned to Jwartan, to say something, although she didn't know what. The serpent's shadow extended even over him, standing several lengths away, protecting him from the harsh daytime suns. He, at least, deserved relief from the heat.

He'd done nothing wrong, only volunteered to accompany Aainah on this journey.

So many years of courtship, so many nights on this exhaustive journey, and yet there he stood, at the end of it all, his back turned on her, just as the rest of their village had done. Just as her own mother had done, when Aainah finally stepped across the threshold into unclaimed territory, bound for the serpent oracle. Jwartan's hands were on his hips, tail decisively raised. Fur rested on his spine in resignation, his posture said as much as his silence. Said all she needed to know. Come back different, it said, or don't come back.

Aainah wholeheartedly agreed.

A chirping sound pulled her attention back to the serpent. Three lines of light appeared on its skin, at the level of Aainah's chest. Like sticks laid in rows, the lines gradually merged together in the direction away from Jwartan.

An invitation.

One last look at Jwartan. Would she see him again? She soaked the sight of him in, his soft grey fur, the lovely bold stripes that zigged across his back. He may have turned on her, as was the custom, but now his ears were slightly, unmistakably tilted in her direction. His plea from their last dusk together, whispered fiercely as they'd curled in shelter against the setting suns, circled in her mind. He'd tell everyone she'd made it through the serpent, if she'd only turn back then. He'd promised. They'd never know.

But she would. And the question would remain. That unnamed question, rooted deep in her gut, consuming her joy before she could even taste it. Sucking the color from her future until it was all but a dry field, bleached in the merciless light of the high suns.

Standing at the tail of the serpent, Aainah was now destined for one thing or the other. To emerge from its Eye a free Onaphi, released from the grip of this restless curse, or to be consumed by the oracle beast. She spoke inwardly to the Third Moon. As the Third endured eternal scorn by the rest of the village, Aainah had always offered it her love, secretly. Quietly. She admired the Third, that it continued to rise night after night, to hold strong its place among its kind, despite the ridicule from her village and likely many others. And now she cast her inner voice out toward the place where the moons hid from the suns. This time, for the first time, she sent a request. She asked for a share of its strength. And its courage.

There was nothing left to do now, but go.

Touching the center line of light on the serpent oracle's side, Aainah found a surprising absence of heat. The pads of her feet crunched dry gravel as she walked in the direction of the converging lines. Nearing the turn of the tail and the unshaded side of the beast, she prepared to bake under the suns, and to keep one eye on the sky. She wondered if the serpent would have her walk the full length of its body sunside, wondered if those who'd never returned hadn't died in the serpent, but had simply been plucked from its side by some lucky predator bird who happened to be scouting the area.

At the very tip of the serpent's enormous tail, only steps from the edge of its shadow, a doorway appeared, suddenly, noiselessly, revealing a darkness deeper even than the serpent's outer skin. Deeper than anything Aainah had ever seen. She stepped inside.

The floor of the serpent's belly was slick, yet dry. Nothing was visible beyond the light cast by the doorway, and that light closed in on itself, shrinking quickly to nothing before Aainah could react. She stood for many breaths, blind, considering her options. She might speak a greeting, or she might simply walk forward. With no other ideas springing to mind, she took a step, followed by another.

Her feet made no sound against the belly of the serpent. Neither did her breath. She stopped to breathe deeply, wrapping her arms around herself. In the soundless void, the rise and fall of her chest offered little comfort. She tried to speak. Pressing a hand to her throat, she felt the vibrations of her neck, as her mouth formed words that amounted to nothing. Had the serpent already decided to consume her, beginning with her voice? Her blood pulsed under her coat, running faster and faster around her insides, as if looking for an escape.

A harsh medicinal scent flooded her nostrils, similar to the crushed herbs the village healer smoothed over cuts, but stronger by multitudes. She doubled over in a fit of silent coughing.

Sharp stabs hit her feet, releasing a chorus of pain. She jumped reflexively, and landed at an odd angle, twisting one leg. She curled into a ball, wrapping her tail around quivering limbs. An urge gripped her mind. To run, to search for the doorway and pound on it, to scream for Jwartan.

But then what?

Would he forgive her foolishness, for undertaking a pointless journey? Would he expect her to be different? Could she pretend to be different?

Fierce itching began at her torso and spread quickly, wrapping around her body until every speck of skin under her fur burned. Attempts to scratch caused the burn to build, until it became something barely tolerable. Was this how the serpent ingested the unworthy?

A wind of cold hit just then, providing a slight relief from the itching. But this wasn't just cold. This was a freeze. Pressing in from all sides, threatening to steal her breath. As if she stood at the highest snow-capped mountain top, all her fur cruelly plucked away. A fleeting wish flashed through her as her mind grew dim. If only she was instead on a mountain top, bird nests be damned, at least she could gaze upon the Third Moon once more, before her body slipped away.

Her thoughts narrowed, iced over along with her body,

slipped from her grasp until there was nothing left but quiet. Nothing but darkness. Deep chill coated in heavy silence. Tipping sideways, she curled as tightly as she could, attempting to trap the last of her body's warmth as cold enveloped her. If this was the end, it had come so soon.

Feeling fell away. Thoughts cracked.

Jwartan's face floated in the near void of her mind, his eyes relaxed, whiskers slanted in the expression he sent her so often, secretly, from across a crowded room, in the way he let her know he was thinking of her. His fur fell away, then, as did his eyes and whiskers, leaving nothing but a gaping emptiness in his grey face, unreadable. Like the Third Moon. She spoke to the moon, then, and also to Jwartan. *If this was the end, it had come too soon.*

Dim light seeped through Aainah's eyelids, although they remained closed. She lay on her side, curled tightly, wondering how many breaths had passed. The cold was gone. Ideas, memories, feelings, all poured back in. A comfortably mild light surrounded her, like that of the Four Moons. Had night arrived? Was she outside? She cracked her eyelids.

She was inside a room, windowless, yet somehow lit by unseen moons, or unseen fire. Floor, walls, and ceiling each curved, one blending into the another, all with the same colorless hue of the serpent's outer skin.

Standing on shaky legs, Aainah noticed the floor give slightly to her step, like soil would. Yet this floor was not a gathering of countless grains, but one complete piece. Circling, Aainah turned her ears in all directions, listening for any sound as she scanned the surroundings. The serpent might have given her light, but sound was still absent.

Why had none of the stories told of what lay within the belly of the serpent? The answer laughed within her. What if they had? What story could she tell, so far? Color absent of color, darker than dark, colder than cold, a noiseless room lighted by absent moons or unseen fire? Her head lightened with the absurdity of it.

Aainah slowed her pacing to stand, waiting to see what the serpent would do next. As if responding, a doorway opened. She stepped through. It led to another room, about the same width, but longer. A light wind kissed the fur on her tail, and the doorway behind her was gone.

Sound flooded in. She could hear herself breathe again. She chuckled. Her voice sounded strange, different than she remembered it. She jumped at the appearance of a shape, on the wall next to her.

It was the size of a grown Onaphi, of Aainah. Through it, she could see the grounds outside the serpent. It was night. The Fourth Moon was visible, grinning large and friendly in the sky as it surveyed the scene. She stepped closer to the opening, just close enough to glimpse the Third Moon. It was small and blank, as usual, its face looking other places. Reminding Aainah that there were other things to see.

Scanning the grounds through the opening, Jwartan was nowhere to be seen. So that was it. He had already left. How many days and nights had passed while she lay frozen inside the serpent?

Aainah reached a hand out and passed it through the opening. The air outside was coarse, draped in dew. This doorway was real. She could leave. She couldn't possibly have reached the eye already, yet the serpent was granting her an exit. Why? Was she cured? No, she was sure she wasn't. She felt like the same Aainah.

It was her mother who'd first recognized Aainah's need for the serpent's healing. Aainah may have hid her sorrow and restlessness from the rest of the village, even from Jwartan, but her mother was in the habit of looking deeper than others felt comfortable. The moment she'd shared her idea with Aainah, that she travel to the oracle and address her pain, the words could not be undone, took on a weight and strength only truth could sustain. Aainah stepped beyond the village's boundary three nights later.

Before turning her back on her daughter, Aainah's mother had whispered her farewell, the red stripes under her chin barely moving as she spoke in the same hushed tone she'd used to tell stories to Aainah long after dawn had broken, while her siblings curled together in contented slumber. As the rest of the Onaphi lined the edge of the village, their backs already turned on Aainah, her mother looked her in the eyes one last time and told her that she would make it through the serpent. All the way to the Eye. And whatever happened then, Aainah would become her true self. Aainah asked her mother, in a voice too small for her body, "but how do you know?" Her mother's only response was a purr, soft and steady—a sound Aainah hadn't heard from her mother in many seasons—as she turned her back on Aainah.

A line of dryness crept across Aainah's arm as she pulled her hand back into the belly of the serpent. She was not done here. The doorway collapsed at the very moment Aainah's hand returned. Shadow appeared in the corner of Aainah's vision. An opening, to another section of the serpent. A familiar tic pulled at Aainah's tail, but she had no interest in suppressing it this time. The jittery feeling it betrayed wasn't annoyance, and definitely wasn't the boredom of village life. It was anticipation. A few quick steps, and she ducked into another room within the belly of the serpent.

As if someone had reached into the sky and covered all moons but the Third, this room was dimmer. The doorway closed behind her.

Like the others, this room was also empty. Or so it seemed, at first. A noise behind her made Aainah jump nearly a full Onaphi length and hit her head against the top of the serpent's body, bending her neck painfully before she fell to the floor.

She stilled, slowed her breathing, and listened. Rustling. Just behind her.

On all fours, tail stiff and ears craned, Aainah turned, and came face-to-face with a child. Small, with a soft pale coat, it crouched against the wall, tail wrapped around its hands and feet. It shivered, although the room did not feel cold to Aainah. She breathed in deeply and found an absence of smell, not only of the child, but also of herself. No whiff of earth caked to her feet, no lingering aroma from the last meal she'd shared with Jwartan.

A black spot decorated the fur around one of the child's eyes, eyes that seemed too serious to belong to a child. All in the Onaphi village bore stripes on their coats. All but one. The only Onaphi Aainah knew with spotted fur was a strange elder, the Counter, who slept outside the door to the village store room, right in the middle of the blazing sunlight, and spent every night with its back bent, counting and re-counting the village's supplies.

Fidgeting and prowling the back rows during village gatherings, as young Onaphi do, the youths would whisper, speculate, suspect the Counter had been birthed in another village, far from their own. This idea remained more story than truth, as adults refused to discuss the matter, and the young were afraid to approach the spotted elder, who only spoke in numbers.

Come to think of it, Aainah was sure the old Onaphi had a black spot over one eye, just like this child.

Aainah relaxed her posture and offered from her throat a soft, pacifying rumble, as she approached the child. It was indeed young. The child hadn't yet grown fangs. How had it survived in the belly of the serpent? Aainah wondered if its language was similar to her own.

"Do you speak, young one?"

In the blink of an eye, the child's shivering ceased. Its tail loosened from its body and raised a few finger-lengths off the floor. Its ears craned toward her. She spoke again, lessening the rumble in her voice, to provide clarity.

"Need help, young one?"

The child visibly relaxed and emitted a mild rumble from its own throat. It was starting to trust her. She took another step forward, but the child slid away in equal measure. Now wanting not to endanger the fragile bond only just formed, Aainah remained where she was and leaned back on her haunches, to match the child's posture.

Stories of Onaphi journeying to the oracle were so few, so old, she hadn't even considered she might find another person within the belly of the serpent, but she supposed it made sense. Other villages must also lay within journeying distance of the serpent oracle. But a child? What sort of village would turn its back on a child? What sort of child would be sent away? It must have been lost. Must have stumbled upon the serpent and hoped for shelter inside, safety from flying predators and baking suns.

The child's tail raised until the tip was visible over its head, as if being startled by a stranger within the body of an enormous serpent was already entirely forgotten, or was something that happened every night.

"Who you are?" Its voice was odd, words confused as a child might do, yet spoken with a clarity that reminded Aainah of a story-teller, of the Onaphi tellers, who stored the lives of all villagers past and present neatly within their minds and let pieces of those lives tumble from their mouths in clear patient tones, to be snapped up by rapt ears and reborn in slumbering dreams.

"Am I?" Aainah's throat rumbled in an attempt, she was aware, to reassure herself as much as this child who was not at all childlike. "I am Aainah."

"Are you, are Aainah, friend?" Its eyes, intent, almost wise, transfixed Aainah. Made the small thing look less and less Onaphi.

Studying the unexpected little one before her, Aainah realized she'd only seen people from other villages a sparse few times in her entire life. She felt her tail raise still and high above her head, as enough questions to fill three store rooms quickly piled up within, waiting at the back of her throat. Controlling her curiosity with some effort, she said, "I am glad to be your friend. If you want."

Purring as it stood, the child walked the few steps between them and bent to nearly meet with Aainah's nose where she sat. Its lack of scent was distracting.

"Aainah friend, come with?"

The child giggled as it evaporated into mist.

Tensing, Aainah turned in tight circles, scanning the room. The child was gone, as was the mist. Her head felt heavy and light at once. Her vision lurched. She stumbled, tripped over nothing but her own confusion, wondered if the child had been snatched by something as unseen as the moons in this place, or if the child had been nothing but a creation of her own mind, a mind that must now be far beyond help's reach.

A breeze tickled the backs of her ears, carrying with it scents. Welcome, familiar aromas. Grounding smells. Of gravel, of weeds and trees. Of Onaphi, one Onaphi in particular. She turned with caution, unsure whether she wanted to lay eyes on the things she sniffed.

He sat in the doorway, posture tentative, wide eyes fixed on her.

"How did you get in here?" She approached the doorway and sat, opposite him.

"I've been waiting outside. It's been two nights." His whiskers trembled. "You look awful."

She surveyed herself, saw what Jwartan saw. Clumps of fur were missing, all over her body, the skin underneath scabbed and abnormally colored. Thoughts slipped from her grasp, scrambled too fast around her mind to be caught. She searched his face. He answered a question she didn't ask.

"A doorway opened. I thought I was imagining it. But then I walked in."

Despite the scents, despite the voice, she wondered if he was real. Unsure what to do, she began counting her breaths, silently, expecting him to disappear into mist after each exhale.

"Is this part, am I part of the serpent's test?"

"Maybe. Yes."

"What has it done to you?" Tears spilled from his eyes.

She reached through the doorway, smoothed the wet fur on his face.

"It's over, isn't it?" His throat rumbled. "Come home with me." He leaned through the doorway and rubbed his cheek against hers, reached for her and pulled her into his embrace. Nuzzling against his neck, she felt everything that was home. Warmth, stories under the light of the Four Moons, savory fish just pulled from the fire, children racing between rooms and wrestling in giggling piles, sparking laughter in even the most serious of elders. Jwartan would always be home to her, all that home could be.

"You're better now. You're fixed, aren't you?"

He was as he always had been, warmth and tradition, just as Aainah realized she was still, she remained, all that she had been.

"It's not finished." She withdrew from his embrace. "I'm not ready."

He stilled. "What's happened in here?"

Words could not explain. "Not enough."

His tail bushed, ears tilted away. "I can't wait forever."

She'd never seen the value in games like this. Especially now, after the freeze, after watching a child vanish before her eyes. "I understand."

His shoulders sank. He looked to one side, maybe toward a doorway. His exit.

"Remember us."

He stood and began walking, his tail dragging on the floor, as the doorway between them collapsed before her eyes. Tears clouded her vision. She'd been too harsh. He hadn't deserved that. A new doorway opened a few steps away. She immediately walked through.

Nothing like the other rooms, this one was lined on either side with what looked like glistening trunks of trees with slick, silvery bark, like a river-buffed rock, nearly sparkling. Like ribs. She was nearing the serpent's head. Nearing its eye.

She walked through the ribs of the serpent.

The shining bones apparently protected no organs, no blood, nothing that she could see. Nothing except her. As she walked, tall windows opened between the ribs. Aainah squinted at the bright midday light that poured into the serpent, almost reaching her feet. Though she could see plant life out there, soaking in the nectar of the suns, no breeze trickled through, no scent of trees or grass.

Sitting beneath a tree was Jwartan, holding out a wide bawn leaf in an attempt to shade his feet. She'd thought he'd be running back to the village, after what he'd said, to join everyone else, everyone who wanted to be there. Yet, despite his hard words, it appeared he was willing to wait, even to sit fully awake, surrounded on all sides by the blaze of high suns. For her.

Aainah watched him as she continued through the serpent's ribs, as he shifted deeper under the tree's cover, until his face was no longer visible. She walked until the sight of Jwartan was well behind her, until she'd nearly reached the other end of the serpent's belly. Until movement outside snagged her attention and pulled her to the window before any thoughts could be formed. Two birds glided toward the tree, toward Jwartan's meager shelter, until they circled above, their wingspans as wide as half the tree's height, their beaks easily larger than an Onaphi head.

Only Jwartan's feet were visible under the bawn leaf, and they didn't move. Clearly he couldn't hear the predators. Maybe he'd fallen asleep. Who wouldn't in the height of day? She screamed his name. Her voice echoed through the belly of the serpent, but clearly didn't escape the oracle. She pressed her hands against the invisible skin of the serpent, the skin that showed her love nearly snatched, nearly eaten. Hard as stone, it didn't budge. She kicked and slammed and snarled as the birds glided down, down, until they were nearly above the top of the tree. They would land soon, on either side of Jwartan. He'd have no way out. He'd die, in the most horrible way, all because of her.

"Let me out!"

The unseen skin covering the window disappeared, and Aainah fell through, screaming his name. Jwartan dropped his leaf shade and stood as the birds hollered, their hunt inter-rupted. They circled tightly and dove toward Aainah, who lay half in and half out of the serpent's window. It was Jwartan who screamed her name this time, told her to run, as he climbed the tree to dive under thicker leaf cover.

The air hissed as it parted, making way for the two birds diving her way. She scrambled backward, back into the serpent, only a body-length away from death when she made it inside and yelled at the serpent to close the window.

One bird reached her before the other. She heard nothing as its beak cracked and shattered against the serpent's invisible skin, now apparently back in place. The second bird steeply turned upward as the first collapsed in front of Aainah, its skull misshapen as blood quickly spilled into the ground. She looked to the tree and saw nothing. Jwartan was safe.

Sinking to the floor and wrapping her tail around her

shaking limbs, Aainah tried to still her panicked heart, soften the gasps escaping her mouth. It was over. All was okay.

But it might not have been. Look what Jwartan had risked, continued to risk. For the sake of someone who barely knew how to love him back.

All the windows within the serpent's belly closed at once, forcing her vision to adjust to the milder lighting. A doorway opened at the end of the room. Only a few steps away. Darkness, deep silence, lay through the door, offering no hint of the next trial that awaited.

The promise of something more sparked anew within her breast, quieting her heart. She would continue. Jwartan's risks would not be for nothing. She walked through the door.

Light raised to a perfect dim. Curiously curved tables scattered around the room and lined its curved walls. The tables were taller than those they built in the villages. They held puzzling shapes, like small tools, attached to their surfaces. Aainah wandered the room, considered whether she should try to touch or move some of the tools. She was examining a table along the far wall when the serpent spoke.

It was the perfection of the voice, ageless, foreign, similar to that of the child but too clear to come from an Onaphi throat, that led Aainah to realize who was speaking. Its words were hard and exact, like a stone smoothed to perfection in a way no Onaphi could ever achieve, in a way only a mighty volcano might accomplish.

"You have done well. Your body is healthy and strong. This means you now have one more choice to make."

Aainah leaped backward when the wall before her sprang to life. It was as if she could see into another serpent's head, an exact copy of the strange room in which she now stood. As if a window had opened to show Aainah not the grounds outside the serpent oracle's body, but another time within its body. It showed other Onaphi, one after another, standing within the serpent, nearly where Aainah herself stood. She looked around to confirm she was alone, yet she looked back to the window to see that no, she was not alone. Despite her head swimming at the experience, nothing could keep her eyes from the stories laid out before her.

A brown Onaphi with white stripes stood before a table. Its mouth and throat moved in words Aainah couldn't hear, and then it walked through a doorway, into a room not much bigger than the Onaphi itself. The eye of the oracle. It leaned against the back wall, its ears in a resting position, as soft and peaceful as those of children in sleep, and the doorway closed. More Onaphi appeared on the screen, one after the other. Some walked into the small room, others left out another doorway, one that led outside. All of them, each Onaphi, when they left, held their tails high and turned their ears forward, intent on their choice. Which of those leaving the serpent had returned to their villages? What happened to those who elected to remain?

The choices of countless Onaphi played out before her. Each chose one of the serpent's Eyes, either stepping into the small room or leaving the serpent's body. Just as Aainah grew accustomed to seeing these scenes that were somehow happening and not happening in the very room where she stood alone, she froze. A face emerged that she recognized. She would know that face anywhere.

Aainah left her mother, an elder, back in the village only a handful of nights ago, yet the Onaphi in the scene before Aainah, with her red striped chin, was also undoubtedly her mother, but with a stronger posture, a fuller coat. Brighter eyes. It was she who'd told Aainah to seek the oracle, she who'd told story upon story of the few who'd made the journey and returned, yet Aainah's mother had never mentioned that she'd walked through the serpent herself.

Aainah held her breath as she watched her mother, so

young, speak silently to the serpent. So very familiar was her mother's face, Aainah thought she could almost make out what she was saying. Almost, but not quite. Of course Aainah knew the choice her mother had made, so long ago. And yet...

Maybe it was because she knew her mother's movements so well that she saw something in the young Onaphi she'd not noticed in the others who'd just chosen their fate before Aainah's eyes. The younger version of her mother had made her choice, had walked through the eye that led outside, and while she held her tail high, Aainah noticed the slightest twitch at its tip. Just once.

Maybe it was from watching her mother so closely during all of her growing up years, to see if her mother would reward her for a job well done or punish her for one of many defiances, that Aainah understood so well the position of her mother's ears. They faced forward, yes, but they weren't as eager, weren't as sure. Not craned fully forward with complete contentment and full acceptance. One ear held back. Tilted, ever so slightly, still trying to soak in the sounds of the serpent her mother had left.

Aainah's mother had always seemed so sure, yet she'd felt regret, back then. Had others been regretful, also? Had those who stepped into the small room felt just as much regret as those who returned to the outside?

"The time is now, Aainah the Onaphi. It is your turn to choose."

Two doorways opened.

"Return to your life, and be assured your visit is greatly appreciated. Choose the other doorway, and you will leave your home, never to return. You will travel to another place, far beyond the stars in your sky, where other creatures wait, happy to be your friend. Some there are Onaphi, most are not. Most will look different, speak different, think different.

"All will be glad to know you."

Aainah's tail fell to the floor. Another place. Not to return.

Jwartan was still outside, waiting. She stepped toward the doorway to see him standing against the tree again, leaning against the trunk. He faced another section of the serpent, his profile strong. His jaw set. The suns cut a sharp angle past the cover of the tree, spilling heat across his back, but he did not move. His devotion was clear. He would endure pain for her, would support her always. She could walk outside, tuck into his embrace, return with him to a shared future within the village. He would accept her, she now realized, exactly as she was. He would never question. But she would.

She was at the end of the serpent oracle's journey, and she was still the same Aainah.

"It is your turn to choose."

Her tail lifted as she soaked in the vision of her Jwartan, standing under meager cover, surrounded by the heat of the blazing suns, waiting for her. She said only two words, quietly. His ears perked, tilted in her direction, followed by his head. They faced each other across the barrier of the serpent, across a distance greater than the number of steps it would take to cross. She closed her eyes and dipped her forehead forward, imagining it meeting Jwartan's.

She left the doorway that led to Jwartan and walked toward the other and through, then leaned against the back wall of the tiny room. The doorway closed in front of her, leaving all but a small section the size of her face, a window. Pressure enveloped her body, holding her still, yet allowing her to breathe. Her tail tried to twitch, but it was held fast, curled around her leg.

Watching through the window, she saw the small room, the eye of the oracle, somehow lifted up, pulled away from the serpent, raised until it was above the serpent's body, as if the eye had grown wings. The tree that sheltered Jwartan was visible for only a second as the land quickly fell away. She couldn't hear her own laughter as birds flew across her vision, apparently unaware of the wonder that was happening at that moment.

She considered, as the land drew away, maybe she'd simply lost her mind. Maybe she still laid frozen just inside the serpent's tail. Another part of her, the part brimming with a joy that swiftly lighted her thoughts, decided it didn't matter. This journey was worth more than four lives in an Onaphi village, real or imagined.

Mountaintops slipped past, as did the searing light of the suns. An enormous gray rock came into view. Though it loomed larger than she could have dreamed, she recognized it immediately. It was the First Moon. Her gut shifted as she curved around its rough backside before moving on to the Second, purple and oddly fogged over. And then the Third lay before her.

She glimpsed its side. Her tail would have twitched like mad if it could have. She was about to see its face. The thing no one saw. The thing her mother told her didn't exist. But then her mother hadn't told her everything. A few breaths passed, and then the face of the Third spread before her. Her heart swarmed, as broken, discordant parts inside of her coalesced, finally, into something that felt whole.

Dark, dimpled, she could see its nose. Its eyes. Facing out. Facing her. Behind the Third was a strange pocked thing, with patches of color and soft clouds drifting over. That must've been her home, where children darted in and out of rooms and birds prowled the sky, where her mother remained. Where Jwartan stood. Yet the Third didn't care about such things. Facing away from the land, away from the mountains, away even from the serpent, the Third only watched the stars.

Aainah now felt pity for her beloved Third Moon, forever stuck in place among its family, unable to accompany her on this indescribable journey. With her inner voice, Aainah thanked the serpent for freeing her, for sending her to a place where she would not be considered wrong.

As the land of the Onaphi and the Third Moon both fell away beneath her feet, she spoke silently. *I will go in your stead, but rest assured. A part of you travels with me.* She relaxed into the serpent's embrace, as countless stars passed before her eyes.

THE ADVENTURES OF WATERBEAR AND MOSS PIGLET

SANDY PARSONS

Deep in the 100 mm petri dish, WaterBear and Moss Piglet played. Light signaled the arrival of Crystal Robin. She had so many fun toys. "What do you think she'll do to us today?" asked Piglet. He was a very timid tardigrade.

"Maybe she'll put us on the Merry-go-Round. We'll get dizzy."

"No, I don't think I'd like that." The last time Crystal had centrifuged them he'd been a tun for weeks. "I'm still trying to get back to my full size."

"I like you the way you are."

Piglet said, "I hope we are always friends."

WaterBear said, "We are tardigrades, we will always be something. But being friends is best."

Crystal was looking at the x-rays from yesterday. "I can see inside your tummy," said Piglet, giggling.

"Is it very Rumbly?" asked WaterBear.

"It's full of agar," said Piglet.

"Oh bother, that must be left over from the last time she smeared us on a slide. I very much wish it were something sweet. Do you happen to have any trehalose in you, perhaps?" WaterBear leaned over and wiggled the hairy ridges which covered his snout.

Piglet hopped sideways. "I'll need it if she freezes us again."

Crystal talked to them while she fed them their lichens and moss and freshened their water. Her favorite stories were about Outer Space. "I bet you guys will be the best astronauts ever. There's nothing you can't survive, so far anyway." Crystal created more games, fire and ice and pressure so nice. She always told the tardigrades what she was doing but the words were long and often muffled by the sound of lichens being chomped. Once, Crystal aerosolized them. WaterBear and Piglet, floating in the ether, waving eight stubby legs at each other. "Look I'm a Roll-y-Poley," said Piglet, rolling into a perfect ball.

WaterBear tried it too, but he was a tubby tardigrade and no matter how much he clenched his paws and scrunched his snout to his bottom he couldn't transform from long into round. He floated with eight claws extended, sailing his body like a kite, riding the waves between particles. When the experiment ended, and he was back in the 100mm petri dish, he felt positively withered, and didn't shuffle or wiggle when Crystal shared the results. "You did so well, my little menagerie. I wish I could boop your cute snoots."

"Did you hear that? She thinks we're cute," said Piglet.

"I don't feel cute. I don't even feel like me today."

Piglet twiddled his front claws. "Do you want some of my trehalose?"

"No thank you. You'll need it for the Big spearmint."

"Wh-what are you talking about?"

"To the stars." WaterBear pointed a claw upwards.

"I don't want to, WaterBear. Here have my trehalose. I'll stay here where its snuggly and moss and lichens are always close to my mouth."

"Well, I won't eat it all, but maybe just a taste?" When he finished, WaterBear hopped and scooted and wiggled until he was puffed out like a tardigrade again. Piglet had gone over to the edge, where the medium thickened, watching Crystal Robin's assistants pack up the laboratory. WaterBear put a paw on Piglet's back, to modulate the shock of the news to his moss piglet buddy. "All of us are going to Outer Space."

"Even Crystal? But how will we get the lichens?" WaterBear tried to answer but Piglet scurried, creating trails through the media. "Maybe we can spell out a message? 'S-o-m-e-t-a-r-d-i-g-r-a-d-e-s!'"

"She already knows we are here." WaterBear put the three paws to his head. "Think of something else. Think. Think."

"How about 'O-u-t-e-r-S-p-a-c-e...N-O-m-o-s-s?'"

But it was too late. Hands clamped a cover on the plate and they jostled and gently sloshed as they settled into a new dark world. Crystal had packed them in foam and the last thing they heard was someone saying, "Rocket Park."

"I will hold your paw, and whatever comes we will be brave together," said WaterBear.

Once the 100mm dish was secured to a conduit on the Flange of the rocket, Crystal opened the lid and snuck a few snacks For the Ride. WaterBear tried to pay attention but he was sleepy from the nanoparticles Crystal's team had spent all week injecting into the tardigrades to track them. They waited a long time for liftoff, Piglet twiddling his claws in between bites of moss and WaterBear taking one last traipse through the 100mm petri dish. Finally, the vibrations signaled the time to leave their Earthly home had come. "Stay by me," said Water-Bear, and they intertwined four sets of claws as the darkness and cold replaced warmth and light. The Flange shook and the conduit opened, and WaterBear and Piglet, media, food and all the other tardigrades floated into the Abyss.

Like reverse popcorn, the tardigrades turned into tuns, but WaterBear, who was even rounder in the middle now, couldn't make his front claws meet the back ones. "Think, think," he said, and Piglet, whose voice was muffled by his body, said "What's wrong, WaterBear?"

"I think I've lost my tail."

"Tardigrades don't have tails, not even you."

"Oh, well then, that's a relief." He was drying out fast, but still couldn't form a ball. Then some space lichen smacked into him and his body reacted as it should. He was a tun, and Piglet floated next to him.

"Where are we going?" asked Piglet.

"I don't know but at least we'll be together."

"Forever?"

"Even longer," said WaterBear.

ISSUE 7

CHANGED BY THE JOURNEY

If you're reading this volume of Zooscape, then you've survived the long, hard spring that lasted ten thousand years. You'll need some provisions before continuing on your journey. So, please, take these stories with you on your way...

Each of these stories is a journey in miniature, and the characters are changed by the end. Much as you may be changed, hopefully for the better, by reading them.

THE GOD-SMOKER

DYLAN CRAINE

"If you do this," said the insect, "then you'll regret it." Her voice had a stentorian quality to it that belied its feeble pitch.

"Oh, I doubt that," said the cheetah. He brought the meerschaum bowl of the pipe closer to his face. "You have no power over me. You may be a goddess to your people, but to mine, you're nothing but a fancy ant." With his other paw, he pushed his teashades up the bridge of his muzzle.

The ant squirmed against the resin that coated the bottom of the bowl. Her legs remained stuck fast. She flicked her wings, but they were no help.

"That's not what I mean," she said. "You think the spiritual potencies you'll gain from consuming me will help you. They won't."

"Hmm," said the cat. He turned the pipe around in his paws, examining the ant-goddess from all angles. As he did, he lay back on the silk couch behind him, his tail flicking out from under his red satin robes. "They won't?" he asked. "There are an awful lot of people waiting past those curtains and down the hall in the auditorium who might think otherwise. They'll be growing impatient soon. They came here to listen to a story. You are—were—a goddess of storytelling."

"So you think that if you reduce me to smoke, and inhale me—"

"I know for a fact." The cheetah smiled a wide, fang-filled smile. "I've done it before. There are thousands of storyteller-deities like you, for all the thousands of insect cultures. For a being of my talent, resources, and determination, it is easy to find you and to capture you. As I have done several times in the past and will do again in the future. So I know from experience that as long as your essence is in my throat, I can create, recall, and recite stories more enthralling and inventive than any mortal could hope to concoct. I've built my career on it, in fact."

As he spoke, the cheetah groped absently for a filigreed fire-lighter that sat on the table beside him. He placed it in his lap, then turned to a drawer in the table and began rooting around in it for the next item he needed.

"You are mistaken," said the ant. "My 'essences' will do no such thing. You tell only the stories you could have told unaided."

"Not likely," said the cheetah, lazily. He retrieved a small bag of shredded leaves, which he dumped over the head of the ant.

"All you'll accomplish," said the ant, "will be to create a build-up of deific-grade prana within your lungs. Eventually, they will refuse to breathe earthly air. You will suffocate yourself—or else live out the rest of your days confined to some minor place of holiness, wheezing and sputtering and questing for those spiritual vapors that might linger, untainted, in the corners of your chapel or shrine. A sad end to a promising storyteller."

A big, black thumb-pad thrust its way into the space beside the ant as the cheetah packed the bowl with the tobacco leaves. He made sure not to injure his captive, but the leaves still pressed uncomfortably against her.

"Please," said the ant, her tone urgent but bitter. "I have done nothing to you. You will gain nothing. You will only hurt yourself."

"They all say that," said the cheetah. He dumped another layer of shredded tobacco over her head. "But I have a performance to put on and a reputation to think of."

She churned her wings to clear space for her head. "So you're a fraud," she said. "Not a true storyteller. You cheat. Is that what you're content to be?"

The cheetah hesitated. He made a show of looking thoughtful. He made a show of looking around himself at the embroidered silk curtains and elaborately-lacquered furniture of the dressing room. Then he said, "Yes, I believe I am content." He smiled again and began to pack the second layer.

"I could tell you a story," she said. "I could tell you a long, sad story about a foolish man who wasted his talent and committed acts of evil and unfathomable stupidity before meeting a strange and bitter end."

He paused, holding the bag of tobacco over her head, ready

to pour the third and final layer. "The story of me," he said. "Or of what you think I am. Why should I listen to it?"

"I could tell that story," said the ant. "If you heard the whole thing, you would feel guilt and horror. You would not do what you are now doing. You would see the truth."

"I wouldn't let you tell it."

"I won't tell it," she said.

"You won't?"

"I won't—but you will. Tonight. To your audience."

The cheetah snorted. "That's not really your decision to make," he said. He filled the rest of the bowl with the tobacco, then began pressing it down around and over her head using his thumb-claw as a tamper. The goddess's compound eyes staring up at him were the last part of her he saw.

He flicked the wheel on his firelighter, hesitated a moment, then lit the pipe.

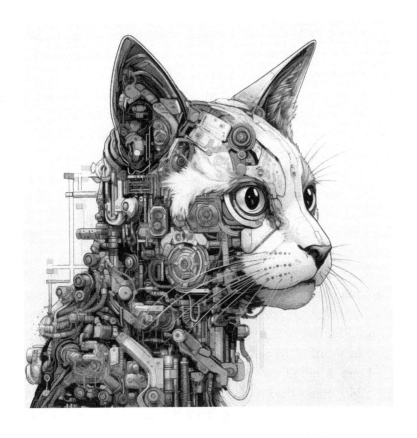

MAKER SPACE

ADELE GARDNER

On his second birthday, Carolina Wannemacher took her son out in his stroller to shop for a new suit. She had instructed him carefully. When the clerk arrived, Nigel lay inert in the harness, just a trifle more still than a soundly sleeping toddler. As Carolina carefully worked the suit onto the artificially stiff limbs, the clerk gave her an odd look. "Are you sure you want to spend the money? A little one like that grows so fast."

"He's a doll, you see," Carolina said seriously, keeping her attention focused on Nigel. He was being so good. Following his programming perfectly. Not an eyelash twitched.

The tag on the clerk's navy blue jacket named her Lotte. She seemed happy with Carolina's explanation. Lotte scarcely even batted an eye when Carolina said she wanted the suits a size too large, as if the doll would grow into them.

When Lotte retreated behind the staff doors, Carolina heard laughter and caught a glimpse of Lotte talking to another clerk. Of course, Lotte would want to share the eccentricities of her client. Carolina took the opportunity to confer with Nigel about his likes and dislikes.

When Lotte returned with several more suits to try, she told Carolina that every woman was entitled to a hobby, and that she herself was making a family of ball-jointed dolls from her favorite fantasy series and sewing the clothes herself. She'd won an award at Dragon Con.

Lotte admired the delicate, realistic modeling of Nigel's face, her finger tracing the weave of the pinstripe on Nigel's baby limbs. Lotte murmured, a wistful note in her voice, "He looks so alive. I wish I knew how you did it."

Carolina smiled slightly. "That's a trade secret."

Lotte's face fell. She drew back, her mouth pinched. "I didn't mean—"

"It's okay," Carolina said. "I've been building prototypes since I was about his size. After a while you just get good at something."

Lotte's face brightened, as if Carolina had said the magic words. "Well, there's hope for me then," she said. And as Carolina made her choices and checked out, Lotte added, "I hope you don't mind, but I wish you'd think about sharing your patterns online. I mean, you're really talented."

Feeling acutely aware of the store camera and Lotte's shy smile, Carolina said, "You might have something there."

She wheeled the stroller onto the sidewalk. Passersby chatted to invisible friends via Bluetooth, but Carolina waited a block before she said, "Good job, Nigel."

"Thanks, Mom."

"I should have done a better job. She actually believed you were a doll."

Those uncannily human blue eyes looked up at her. "Don't worry, Mom, you did the best you could."

"Next birthday, Nigel. Next birthday I'll do better, I promise."

"Can we have friends over? I'd like to invite Audrey. She seems nice."

Carolina fell silent as a man in a business suit passed her with a half-smiling nod, which she returned gravely. She considered. Audrey was fifteen, an online pal of Nigel's, compatible in many ways. Home-schooled, a child prodigy who played cello with the symphony, Audrey would probably sympathize with Nigel's differences from other children, especially his advanced intelligence. But she was sheltered, and quite close to her mom. Was it wise to trust her with the secret?

Nigel was a healthy, growing boy, but arranging playdates was difficult. Though plenty of adults in Carolina's generation had been enthusiastically building robots since they were tiny tots receiving their robotics and circuits kits from Santa, most of these were far more limited than Nigel. Carolina didn't want to reveal just how advanced he was. And the human kids who might be more intellectually compatible carried too much risk of letting the cat out of the bag.

At her continued silence, a cloud passed over Nigel's face. "Mom? Her cello sounds so beautiful with my harpsichord. I thought we might have a concert."

Her heart hurt. Was she doing right by him? He looked up at her with such trust in that little-boy face, his skin as creamy as her own, his hair in blond curls modeled on her little brother's at that age. "She's a little young for you, honey. Maybe next year. A lot of girls mature when they turn sixteen."

Nigel sighed, a mannerism he'd picked up from her. But he settled back in the stroller contentedly enough. He started humming Jean-Philippe Rameau's *Pièces de Clavecins en Concert*, performing both the harpsichord and cello parts, adding improvisations in the baroque style and harmonizing with himself, his tripled and quadrupled voice eerie and beautiful in his perfect, little-boy pitch.

Buying a suit had been his birthday wish. He wanted to follow Audrey's lead and take up the traditional position of the child prodigy, sharing his skills with an audience, even if only a virtual one. He was too young to be self-conscious enough for stage fright. He didn't even know he should be scared.

Or what he, her robot child, had to fear.

CAROLINA WANNEMACHER WORKED at Hilliard Public Library and lived with five cats, who loved her fiercely and followed her from room to room with loud purrs, rubbing her legs and nuzzling her feet and ankles.

The library was good to her. She enjoyed the supportive, creative atmosphere. Among the treats she prized most was the chance to lead and attend Maker programs. Coding, robotics, 3-D printing—she had plenty of skills to share with their patrons. Carolina had been designing robots since childhood. Her son Nigel was the great project of her life, and she built him in the Maker Spaces of many libraries. She was careful to create only individual parts at each location, staying within the printing limits per patron while avoiding anyone guessing what she built.

Each year she made Nigel a new birthday suit, a human frame one developmental step up from his prior body, with an expanded brain to match. She reasoned that his best chance to acquire not just sentience but wisdom would be to start as a little child, then grow as any human would. She'd teach him all she could about what was good in life, how to love, what mistakes to avoid; she'd share memories of family and the best of human culture. She wanted him to have the chance to appreciate this wonderful life, not simply receive a data dump. The best way she knew to create depth was the same lifetime commitment her parents had made to her.

When Nigel was five, he told her that for his next birthday present, he wanted to be a cat. She smiled and pretended surprise. Though she wondered if it was a good idea at this developmental stage, she loved cats and preferred their company to that of most humans. Her five cats were highly affectionate, creative, and intelligent, and Nigel needed to build his socialization skills.

Human science had come a long way in translating the complex speech of fellow Earthlings, but with at least as many multisensory as verbal cues, Cat was a tough nut to crack. Carolina started with a translation algorithm based on the latest in talking cat collars from Japan and added data from veterinarians, cat behaviorists, and her own experience. Maybe Nigel could fill in some of the blanks.

Nigel loved being a cat. Carolina had thought he would. He'd been romping with the cats on all fours since birth; in many ways, he grew up speaking Cat. He chose to be a calico female whom he named Duchess. Carolina let him help sculpt the details, just as she'd helped her grandma quilt when she was little.

Though she equipped Duchess with a voice synthesizer for human speech, the new calico sported all the feline communication devices—vocal, olfactory, tactile, and body language. When Duchess talked to Carolina, the other cats shied away from the mysterious human voice issuing from the cat's body.

Soon Duchess lifted her furry chin, held her whiskers high, and spoke to Carolina only in Cat with other felines present.

Duchess imitated the other cats, learning the delicate language of touch and brush, the infinite meanings in the quirk of a whisker. She palled around, tangled with them, snuggled and slept with them. She shared their food, water, and litter-boxes as part of the cat communications network.

Carolina worried at first that Duchess needed more intellectual stimulation, both for education and entertainment, but her child pleaded earnestly for the Cat Immersion Experience. Being a cat was a full-time job.

Embracing the cats' Eternal Present, Duchess joined in group grooming, cleaning Moonie's ears, then submitting to Sebastian's face-wash. She formed part of the patchwork fur pattern when the cats curled in a sunny heap, nestling her chin in Cleo's side while Rocco draped his arm across her back. In the evenings, Duchess rushed with all the cats to greet Carolina and sit with her. It felt strange at first to stroke her child's silky head and scratch around cat ears and chin, but Duchess purred, looking up at Carolina with a cat's pure love.

One day, when Carolina tossed tiny toy mice and fishes, Max's acrobatic leap landed him on Duchess's back. Duchess yowled in pain and flattened to the ground. Carolina ran over and scooped her up. Not for the first time as a robot's mother, worry smote Carolina. To fit all of Nigel's boy-sized brain in the cat, Carolina had positioned parts in places normally reserved for internal organs. "Baby, are you all right?"

Duchess meowed a complaint. What to do? No emergency vet would treat a robot cat.

Talking to Duchess soothingly—she always kept her cats informed—Carolina said, "Don't worry, Duchess. I'm just going to do some diagnostics. Make sure everything's okay."

Duchess issued a raspy protest; her claws lightly pricked Carolina's arm. Carolina ignored this, stroking her synthetic fur as she hooked Duchess up. Rocco ran over to check on the calico, who hid her face in Rocco's ruff.

Fortunately, the spine had protected the brain, as it should. But when Carolina released the calico, Duchess skittered away, then ignored Carolina, grooming herself with total concentration as if the examination had been an affront to feline dignity.

Carolina's anxiety did not disperse as easily. She'd been too lax. Introducing a robot into a clowder of cats might be just as dangerous as it was fun. Now that she looked more sharply, she thought Moonie might be losing weight. Maybe he'd just been playing extra hard with a sixth cat in the house, or faced too much competition for food. She hovered, making sure the big cats didn't chase him from his bowl. But Moonie ate less and less, though he still ran to her when she dished out wet food.

No one could discover what was wrong. The specialist prescribed medicines against every possible illness; this only made his appetite worse. Carolina dropped everything to care for him, but he slipped through her fingers like water.

The other cats worried. Whenever Moonie emerged from Carolina's cat-hospital bedroom, they washed him, touched noses, and snuggled close, offering comfort. Duchess followed Moonie everywhere. Carolina took her child aside, holding Duchess on her shoulder and petting her while she explained how sick Moonie was. Duchess purred into Carolina's ear. The little calico licked Carolina's face.

Then, all at once, there was no more time. Packing Moonie in his carrier for the emergency vet, she walked him around to the other cats for a chance to say goodbye, just in case. But he couldn't be saved. Too much had gone wrong. Carolina sang to Moonie as he died.

When she returned, her weeping scared the cats away. She wanted to explain to Duchess, at least. With wide eyes, laid-back ears, and puffy tail, Duchess looked thoroughly spooked.

The little calico hid her head in Carolina's armpit while Rocco howled from the kitchen, hunting for his missing friend.

By night, Duchess curled in a tight little ball against her side. By day, Duchess followed Carolina as if afraid to let her out of sight. Duchess let her batteries run low, though Nigel had been responsibly charging himself since he was four. Carolina began plugging Duchess in while the calico hunkered beneath the desk—one of Moonie's favorite spots. How horrible grief must be for a cat, who lived in the Eternal Present, where there was nothing but this love, this loss. A cat couldn't distract the grief with a book, TV, or solid work. Duchess seemed exhausted by it, pressed down to the ground by an overwhelming force of gravity.

At last Carolina took action. She returned Duchess to Nigel's most recent body—she always saved the last two for emergency spares. The six-year-old robot boy wouldn't speak. Carolina held him on her lap and stroked his hair and spoke to him softly about their friend Moonie, how much they missed him, and how unfair it was that cats should have such brief lives, their great hearts leaving little record on this earth except in the hearts that loved them. Nigel cried with her, silently at first. At last he whispered, "Please, Mom, I want to be a girl now."

"That's fine, honey." Carolina set to work. She thought she understood: it would be both a reminder of his life as a cat, and a complete switch from the life he'd known, which had been flipped upside down by death.

And maybe, just maybe, it showed a desire to get closer to her. For that was the year they started to truly bond, as Duchess had done with her fellow cats. With relief, Carolina found that this continued, even after Nigel returned to being a boy.

∼

YEAR BY YEAR, Nigel had gone to his body fittings without complaint. Carolina tried not to let him see how she worried. So many things might go wrong during the annual transfer. She backed him up on several computers, but that wasn't his consciousness—she couldn't duplicate that spark. There was only one Nigel Wannemacher in the universe.

Near the end of each year's body, Nigel moved more slowly. He looked listless, dispirited, sick: too much wear and tear on the joints, the body materials grown fragile, not enough energy. He limped. He called for her in the night, terrified, though usually his dreams delighted him—the stranger, the better. Carolina considered turning off the dreaming module, though she considered it essential to an artificial human intelligence. With the dreams came imagination, poetry, playing pretend, and flights of fancy she'd never achieved for the logic-bound robots of her youth. Nigel *felt* the novels he read, rather than simply understanding or analyzing them.

She had to do more to help him. Her funds meagre, Carolina ranged farther afield to take turns in the Maker Spaces of more libraries. She tried pushing up the replacement schedule, working hard to create parts and make him a full body faster, proactively substituting components before they had a chance to wear down. To raise funds for more parts, she finally began licensing her designs, concealing herself behind a handle.

Still, as his ninth birthday approached, Nigel dragged as if his body had grown too heavy. He stayed cheerful, but his patient weariness reminded Carolina too much of lost loved ones in their last days. "Nigel, are you feeling bad?"

"No, Mom." He never liked to complain. He was like the cats that way. But she had deliberately built him without a poker face. Expressions were too valuable in human communications.

Carolina observed, "You don't look well."

"I'm all right, Mom." Carefully, he took a seat at the dining room table.

She pulled out a yellow chair and joined him. "You seem tired. I'd like to run some tests."

"I don't need any tests." His realistic silicone face looked worried, drawn in.

She sat him down that afternoon and plugged in nodes and wires. He fidgeted. He asked to leave. As she dialed him back toward sleep, he lay in the chair lethargically. She offered to replace a ball bearing in his elbow that was generating a low level of background pain. His normally pale skin took on a greenish tinge closer to Mr. Spock's than she'd ever achieved with her mother's eyeshadow at Halloween.

She knelt beside him, stroking his arm. "What's wrong, Son? Does it hurt you when I run these tests? Or when I replace your parts?"

His voice was as small as that of any young boy trying to be brave. "Not as such."

She said, "But something about it—upsets you?"

"Disquiets," he whispered.

"Frightens?"

He did not answer. Dread was written all over his face.

"What happens to you when I change your body?"

The answer was simple, stark. "It feels like dying."

Why had she never asked this before? Heart in her mouth, hand on his, she asked Nigel, "Are you awake the whole time? What are you aware of?"

His voice distant, Nigel said, "Fire cuts me out of my body, like having my limbs cut off by a welding torch. I'm left in a tiny prison. I have no eyes, but I can peer out through the cracks."

"The camera on my computer terminal," Carolina whispered.

Nigel's voice sounded tinny. "I can't get out. While I'm stuck there, nothing exists but the moment of consciousness. I am trapped there for a very, very long time. Forever."

With a pang, Carolina thought of that Eternal Present he'd shared with the cats, which made a cat's suffering so unendurable. And yet they so patiently bore it. Like Nigel.

"Why didn't you tell me?"

"I love you, Mom. I didn't want you to worry."

"I'm already worried. Tell me," she urged him, her throat tight. She listened with a sinking feeling.

"Suffocation is not the right word," he said. "There's a complete lack of air and life—like suddenly being snuffed out —as though the world is far away, down a long, dark tunnel—I can't stretch far enough to reach the light—I'm fading away like Moonie—" His voice faded, too. He stopped, his mouth twitching.

Carolina said at last, "I'm so sorry, Nigel. I wish I had known. I'll find some way to fix it. Thank you for being so brave." She hugged him, feeling desperate at her helplessness.

Now as she designed and planned, she sought Nigel's feedback; they worked on improvements together. They perfected a technique of connecting him to a new body or parts before disconnecting the old, and having him make the leap himself. But the basic problem remained: Carolina needed to construct her son out of sturdier materials. After several years of hard work, she earned her fourth degree and got a job at the library of a space science laboratory, where she negotiated limited use of their 3-D printers as part of her compensation package.

By now, many others were building robots based on her original designs. This community shared their research and problem-solving. And the climate around robotics had changed enough that Carolina began to participate in interviews—online, of course, under her handle. She earned additional funds to help Nigel by writing articles. She still worried that someone might come after him; she protected their privacy. But she did reveal a few facts. People were initially surprised to learn she was a librarian rather than an engineer, but they smiled when they read about her Triple Nine IQ.

Without intending to, Carolina found she'd inspired a movement. The passionate advocacy for robot rights proved helpful: when fifteen-year-old Nigel completed the online coursework for his PhD, rather than incur a storm of protest, the university passed a memorandum that recognized that a degree-earning "identity" might be artificially constructed. Then Nigel aced his astronaut exam. But despite NASA's enthusiasm for his potential, he was still legally property, not a person, and could only go to space if Carolina "sold" him to the government. Instead, he took up robotics, going even farther than Carolina, who loved the field, but deeply enjoyed her library career, which unified her disparate interests and intellectual talents perfectly. Her greatest pleasures were an afternoon devoted to reading a good book while listening to classical or jazz and snuggling with her cats, or having an intellectual conversation with her son and protégé, who often contradicted her in the most intriguing ways.

As ocean levels rose and devastating storms increased, many robots stepped forward to help, providing invaluable rescue efforts and dyke repairs. Many robots selflessly gave their lives. Their mourning human families made it abundantly clear that the robots had acted on their own initiative. The footage went viral.

NASA eloquently pleaded the robots' cause; indeed, Nigel's research showed how essential the robots' skills would be in preparing other planets for human habitation. Congress created a conditional proposal. With fear for human jobs and resources on the overcrowded Earth, robots might be granted U.S. citizenship provided they agreed to go to space and fulfill the missions NASA designed.

Nigel told her his plan, as nervous as any young person

about to leave home for the first time. She smoothed his blond curls, kissed his creamy cheek. "You're everything a son should be. Everything I ever dreamed of in a family. My little boy," she said. "I'm so proud of you."

His dimpled chin and worried frown, so similar to her dad's, expressed more concern for her than himself. "Do you want me to stay with you, Mom?"

It wrenched, but she said it: "No, pursue your dreams."

The first step was a mission to the moon. Nigel's face lit up, his blue eyes glowing with starlight, a new feature she'd given him for his seventeenth birthday. Though he did his own design work now, he accepted her gifts for old times' sake. Carolina saw him off with other robots and their human parents, her heart lifting to see this rainbow of human and robot diversity united in one proud moment.

The mission gave NASA a chance to show off the value of their all-robot crew. With few physical needs, the robots made great progress on the construction of the moon base, including a shielded shelter, greenhouse, and oxygen extraction facilities. On the return voyage, NASA broke the good news—new laws prohibited discrimination against artificial versus biological humans. Nor would the robots have to be exiled to earn their citizenship. It only made sense: with so many humans already benefiting from artificial limbs and organs, imposing legal limits on humanity would raise too many problems.

As his departure for Mars neared, Carolina realized that Nigel's dream would be her greatest nightmare. She might never see him again. From the moment she'd created him, he'd been his own, not hers. She wanted above all else for him to be happy. But she had to make sure he was doing it for the right reasons. "You're my family, Nigel. I didn't build you so you would sacrifice yourself for us."

"I know," Nigel said gently. "You gave me free will—that's why I'm doing it. I love you, Mom." He hugged her. "That's why

I want to save you! You and the human species. To make sure you'll live on, I have to make sure there's still a future for humanity. And a future for Earth, so you can keep doing what you love." His voice broke, splitting off into harmonics, dividing into the individual notes she'd braided to create his adult baritone.

"But Nigel—" She floundered, then decided to just say it. "That's beautiful, but what I'd love most is to continue to share our lives! We're not just family, we're best friends. Not to mention scientific partners."

"I'll still be doing our work—putting our research in action. They need me out there. Robots can survive the elements better. We have less complicated atmospheric and sustenance needs. If we can tweak Mars to create a more hospitable environment for humans, colonization can begin in earnest. Then, with some of the pressure off Earth's ecosystem, the planet will begin to bounce back."

Carolina flushed. She found herself arguing against a plan she admired in theory. "But you're not a farmer. That's essentially what you'd be—a space farmer, harnessing the natural environment, moving water around for the benefit of crops like trees. I love trees. But you'll be bored out of your mind!"

His eyes twinkled. "Admit it. You worried about the same thing when I became a cat. But that's not how life is for me. I find the minutest detail interesting. And I can compose a sonnet in my head about the joy of having whiskers or the glory of a sunrise on Mars, then store it and call it up again later to tinker with while I'm drilling for water or sculpting mountains into underground cities. One thing the cats taught me: to savor the moment. I can see the stars shining in the day." He smiled. "You gave me that, Mom." He laid a gentle hand on her shoulder.

She looked out the window, at the sun shining on all that green. Virginia summers—so hot, but so very beautiful. "You could also do a lot of good here," Carolina said. "If you want to help, why not stay and clean up the environment or revive endangered species? Or you could be a poet. A deep sea diver. A veterinarian. A university professor. A ballet dancer. A concert harpsichordist," she urged. "Anything you set your mind to!"

"Oh, Mom," he said fondly.

So she took a deep breath and told him her own news. "I guess I'll be seeing you on the red planet then," she said, and grinned at his surprise. "NASA offered me and the other families first refusal on the human missions, provided we pass the tests. Maybe I'll found the first library on Mars." Exhilarating thought! Visions of library spires danced against red cliffs.

Of course, NASA couldn't afford to send dead weight to Mars, despite her robotics expertise. She'd have to embark on yet another degree program and more training. But fortunately, fifty-two was the new twenty, and she loved to learn. She'd work it in around her library schedule. By the time she was ready to go, he'd be ready to welcome her. And she'd have had time to plan and advocate for the library she'd bring.

Carolina continued, "We won't see each other right away." She chose to look at the bright side, the way Dad taught her. "But we can collaborate. And it'll be so exciting to be working toward the same goal."

He said, "Who knows, by the time you join me, maybe we'll have it looking like Bradbury's small-town Martian paradise."

She reflected. "That *would* be the time to build a library." She floated on the delicious thought of all those novels and movies and music, art and oral histories, scientific texts and poems from around the world, in a wide variety of formats. "We'll need a Maker Space," she concluded.

"Yes!" he agreed. His eyes twinkled. "Highly appropriate— for two Machers in Space."

She laughed. "My dad would have loved that pun."

As they moved into the living room, Sebastian and Max wove between their legs and meowed. Despite his age, Rocco wrestled his way to the top of the cat tower to purr into her ear.

"Cats. We'll need cats," Carolina said.

Nigel beamed. "That, most of all."

WHEN THE HORSE CAME TO THE OPEN HOUSE

K. C. MEAD-BREWER

No one gave it a second thought. Lots of people attend Open House events for the free cookies or wine, or maybe just to admire a stranger's shiplap and crown molding, bathroom mirrors in the shapes of seashells. No, the neighborhood didn't begin to worry until a few days later when the zippy little realtor came out of the house smiling at the horse and the horse nodding back at him.

What does a horse want with the house on the corner? It

normally wouldn't be a big deal except that more than a few people in the neighborhood are allergic to hay and the horse's (truly exceptional) diamond shoes keep cracking the sidewalk.

"Her head weighs the same as my entire brother!" the Lightfoot's girl was heard whispering to another. The neighborhood children are mystified by all the new horse-facts they're learning now. (It never really occurred to them to look up horse stuff before.) How much does a horse heart weigh? How much do horses poop? Has a horse ever been to outer-space? How many lungs do horses have? Are horses good at keeping secrets?

～

THEY BEGIN to wonder if the horse might be keeping secrets.

～

SPYING children must be startled off the horse's porch like birds nearly every day now. The clever ones have started throwing toys over the horse's fence for the excuse to climb into her yard and fetch them.

Scaling her fence, the children look in upon the lushest garden: all kinds of lettuces, lumpy rainbow tomatoes, an apple tree dotted with tiny red and yellow apples, strange herbs with sticky leaves, and a long row of—one of the Robertson girls calls it right away, probably thanks to all those Girl Empowerment camps where they learn about medicinal plants and old myths and—rampion. "It's also known as Rapunzel," she explains with some importance.

They try to remember how long the horse's mane is, if they could use it to climb a tower. They begin to wonder if a horse can also be a witch. (Perhaps this is one of her secrets.)

The children hush each other as they explore the horse's

garden, smelling its savory muds and fruits, looking for things to steal. Instead they find themselves wondering where all these other trees came from and what about those rain-slicked boulders and how long have they been walking?

～

AS YOU MIGHT IMAGINE, the neighborhood parents want to know what's become of their children.

"Where did you leave them?" the horse replies. "Next time try stacking them like the books at the library. Alphabetical order is so reassuring, don't you think? Like a smile full of strong, healthy teeth."

The horse bares her great teeth in example, but it isn't at all reassuring to the parents.

The parents wander the neighborhood that's suddenly empty of their children, the planned and unplanned offspring they built their lives around. They can't remember their own Open Houses or why they settled here. They weren't trained for this. They weren't prepared to think of themselves as their own future.

"What now?" they ask back and forth, a desperate echolocation. "What now?" "What now?"

～

THE CHILDREN AGE as they venture deeper into the horse's garden, deeper and deeper until they come out the other side and discover themselves on the moon.

"This sure isn't Kansas," they joke, turning in circles. They're as tall as adults now, muscled and boobed and hairy. They hold hands, they kiss. They smell like old bedsheets.

Examining their dusty path, they realize the moon's craters aren't craters at all but ancient hoofprints.

It never occurred to them to wonder where horses came from before Earth, nor what it might be like to live on the moon. Will they need special shoes? Will they meet many astronauts? When did the horses first leave the moon, and has it always been this lovely? Its shadows so deep and gentle? Its dirt so soft and cool?

They begin to wonder if they might have secret knowledge of their own now, to find so much promise in a world that others have left for dead.

LOVE FROM GOLDIE

DAVID STEFFEN

We used to be so close. What happened between us, Gloria? Is it because I died? I would never have thought our marriage was so superficial. For Christ's sake, we'd been married for eighteen years! And now you won't even talk to me, won't even look at me. I'd never even believed in reincarnation, but here I am. I guess reincarnation believed in me.

I know I've changed. You pass by and I watch you, unblinking, hoping for even a split second of eye contact. After being ignored for so long, even that small acknowledgment of my existence would be amazing. But, no, you keep walking. As always.

You look so close, yet we are separated by compressed infinity. The entrance on top of my prison is open, always enticing me, but outside I cannot breathe and a terrible gravity holds me down.

I push towards you again, but the invisible barrier holds me back. You still don't look at me, but you approach me and rain flakes of disgusting nourishment down upon me. And I grudgingly gobble them up, resentful of my betraying hunger.

Breakfast passes in silence as you read your newspaper and I watch. If only I could read it too, but the headlines are distorted into nonsense shapes, like a reflection in a funhouse mirror.

Soon you leave for work, and I have nothing to do until you return. My new life is so empty when I'm alone. Is this how you felt when deadlines loomed and I had to work overtime, my presence only evident by my incoming paychecks?

I return to my abode and marvel for the hundredth time at the beauty of its façade. It is a cruel trick, but one which I allow myself to fall for time and again. The outside is wondrous, a rainbow of colors: my castle, my home, promising even greater splendor and luxury inside. But once across the threshold, the lie is revealed. The inside is colorless, featureless, nothing but a hollow shell, the discarded skin of a mythical beast. Yet it is my only refuge from the light. In here I can forget what I've become for a time, and can remember happier times.

My favorite memories are our trips together, once every year, a different location every time. Backpacking across Europe, volunteering in South Africa. My favorite trip was Australia, and diving by the Great Barrier Reef. The vibrant colors, the lush wildlife, all existing there as it had long before people ever came across it. How I longed to be one of those fish, living there forever in an underwater wonderland with you.

I float in the dark and remember until I can stand it no more, and I retreat from my castle. But it is equally dark outside. Has the sun already set? You should have been home long before now. I hope you didn't get in a car accident on your way home.

I wait and wait until I feel I will die from the anticipation. Finally, I see the door from the garage open and you come in, alive and well, thank God! And you're... with someone. A man. And... you're holding hands.

Gloria, what are you doing, bringing a man into my house? But I suppose it's not my house anymore, and you are free to do what you like. I don't even know how long it's been since I died. Maybe you waited a respectful amount of time. I can't bring myself to look away as you kiss him, long and wet.

I grow agitated as I watch the kiss go on and on and I work myself into a froth, spinning round and round in my confinement. I spiral up and up and I escape. I try to run to you, to shout to you, but the poison air and crushing gravity assault me, leaving me pathetically stranded, barely able to move.

I succeed in interrupting your kiss, and you scoop me up in your hands—oh the ecstasy of your touch, the feel of your skin against mine—and then you dump me unceremoniously into my prison without a word.

You wash your hands, and then you grab him by the shirt and pull him along after you, toward the bedroom, our brief but intimate encounter already forgotten. I am thankful, at least, that I don't have to watch what happens next.

"I love you, Gloria," I try to say, but there is no sound, only bubbles rising before my eyes.

RIDING THROUGH THE DESERT

LAURENCE RAPHAEL BROTHERS

On the third day in the desert, we stopped at a dusty old creek bed full of drift sand. I was hoping we could dig a shallow well but— "No dice," said my horse, so we moved on.

I sighed. "At least we're out of the rain."

"Rain," he said, shaking his head, "Come on, Susannah, don't torture me like that."

"Sorry."

We kept going. Pioche, Nevada was supposed to be out here somewhere, said to be the last outpost of humanity in the sprawling desert covering the western half of the former United States. The change was supposed to have started around here, and the people in Pioche might have clues to reversing it. Or maybe we could call for help from the space aliens who were supposed to have landed nearby back in the day, at a place called Area 51. Both were feeble hopes, to be sure, probably no more than hoaxes or myths from a hundred years ago, but we had nothing left to us back east.

Before the change this had been scrub land, dry but livable, but now it was a barren mix of salt flats and sandy dunes. With the exception of some black specks overhead that were probably rocs or teratorns keeping watch in case we should stop moving, there was no visible sign of life, not even a cactus or a tumbleweed.

"Break time," I said after a while. "Okay?"

"Sure thing, Sooz." My horse formed a nipple for me in the back of his neck, just behind his silvery mane, and I sipped some of his water.

Later that night, we made a rough camp in the middle of nowhere. Since there were never any clouds or haze, the stars shone like rhinestones and the milky way shimmered overhead. My horse stood a few yards off, looking up at the sky. I wondered what he saw there, how it affected him. After a minute, he shook his head like he'd decided something, and turned to face me.

"Something's out there," he said.

"Really? You think so?"

"In the desert. It's like it's calling to me."

I looked in his big blue eyes, put my hand on the soft skin above his nose, felt his warm breath on my cheek. Just like a regular old horse, which was pretty much the opposite of what he was.

"What about you?" he asked. "You got any feel for what's out there?"

"Nope," I said. "But I'm not a magical horse critter, either."

He sighed and I petted him on the nose again. "I'm sorry, horse. Wish you didn't have to slog all the way out here with me. I know how hard it is on you with no water around anywhere."

"Come on, Sooz. Can't hardly be your horse no more if we split up, now can I?"

I hugged him tight around his neck, buried my face in his mane. "Damn it, horse, don't you make me cry."

He snorted. "Shouldn't waste the water. Case you were wondering, that's why I'm still standing here on four legs stead of hugging you back the way I want to. Takes too much water for me to change right now. Got to conserve."

"Oh. How much do you have left?"

"Three-four days at this rate."

"That's all?"

"Yeah. This place's as dry as I've ever been. You know I can dowse like anything, but it ain't working here."

"Shit," I said. "It's not your fault. It's just— it's not right the way you're always doing everything for me. I don't feel right about riding you, even."

My horse shook his head and pulled his lips back a little from his big yellow teeth. "I go where you go. No matter what. Unless you want me to leave."

"Oh no," I said. "Not ever. I know when I got it good."

"So why don't you bind me?" he asked. "Then it really would be forever. And you could use my name, too, 'stead of just calling me horse."

I sighed. "We've been through that. It's not fair. You'd have to do whatever I said and—"

"I'd like that, though."

"Damn it, horse, you know I wouldn't. And that's why I can't use your name, with you unbound, because maybe someone would hear me say it, and then *they'd* be the one to bind you."

"I guess it makes sense," he said. "I just— Well, let's see what happens tomorrow. We'll find the place for sure."

But we didn't. Just more desert. We started spiraling out from the place we thought Pioche should have been, looking for something, anything at all, and not finding it. On day six, we played dead for half an hour, and lured a pair of teratorns out of the sky, change-born birds so big they shouldn't have been able to fly, but that didn't stop them any more than being impossible stopped my horse. I got the first one with my revolver while it was considering who to take a bite out of first, and then I had to pull out my Winchester and waste a precious 30-06 cartridge on the other when it took off. My horse drained the water out of the birds in under a minute, leaving dried out husks behind.

"How much?" I asked.

"'Nother day's worth, maybe."

There were no more black specks in the sky after that.

I kind of lost track of time then because I wasn't taking near as much water as before, and I think it was making me a little crazy. Everything was hurting, especially my head and my throat. My next drink was the only thing I could think about, after a while.

It was day eight, past midnight, when my horse staggered and fell. It was either luck or him trying to spare me, because I didn't get my leg crushed even though I wasn't paying attention to my riding. I had to help him up, and it was scary-easy to do; he weighed no more than me by then. And where he used to be a silver-tone gray with a coat so rich it was almost like a cat's, now he was pale, bleached white, and I could see his bones under his skin. I felt terrible, because I hadn't noticed how bad off he was, wrapped up as I was in my own misery.

"I'm sorry," he said, "I just can't anymore."

The shame in his voice woke me up from the fevered trance I'd been in, and it made me as angry as I'd ever been. Angry at myself, really, but I didn't want to admit it.

"You big old idiot!" I shouted at him, though it made my throat hurt even worse. "Why'n't you tell me you were out of water?"

"You know why," he said.

"Damn you. You think I want to leave you behind?"

"You got to."

"Well, I'm not going to. You better take some water from me, and we'll go on together till we both can't anymore."

"From you? No way—"

"Listen," I said, "I know you love me. I do, okay? But you got to admit I love you too. So for once, let me be the one to give you something."

"But—"

"God *damn*, horse, do what I tell you."

I thought I was dying, but for his sake I didn't cry out or flinch, even though I could feel the water draining out of my blood and muscles and guts and eyes and everything. But he started filling out a little, getting a touch of color back in his coat, so that was okay, and when he was done, I was still standing, so that was okay too.

We walked on, side by side, me leaning on him, and I don't know which of us was slowing the other down, but it wasn't exactly speedy travel. Then the sun came up, and all I saw in four directions was the hazy flat desert horizon.

"Camp?" asked my horse.

"Nah," I said, choking on the words. "No point."

The sun was halfway up to the zenith, and it was already hot as hell and way drier, when my horse shuddered. I thought he was going to collapse again, but he raised his head and I could see his sunken blue eyes gazing fiercely off to the west.

"Water," he said. "That way. If I ain't crazy, anyhow."

I looked, but it was all flat dry sandy nothing. Any other time I'd give him shit, but not today. So we changed course and kept going.

Noon. We were neither of us going to last much longer, and I was wondering if it was okay to just quit. But my horse was still trudging onward, and I decided I'd be damned if I gave up before he did. And just like that, there it was, a big old crater not more than a hundred yards away. I was on my last legs, sure, and so was my horse, but no way could we have missed seeing it from miles off. We went up to the lip and there was just a shallow grade down to the crater floor, and half a mile away a cluster of small structures.

It took us a good fifteen minutes to make it that far. The town wasn't much, a dozen clapboard buildings. That was strange, because where'd they get the wood from anyway, but just then neither of us was wasting time on little things like that. My map said Pioche was supposed to have a couple hundred buildings spread out over a few square miles of ground, but then it was a pre-change map, so who knew, anyway.

My horse said "Water: there," and *there* turned out to be an old-timey trough with a lever pump beside it. And don't you know it pulled water on the first swing of the handle? Yeah, right, impossible, except we were both head-down in the trough drinking the impossible water instead of arguing with it.

Half an hour later, I recovered enough to realize how messed up I'd been, and how close to dying. My head was pounding, I had the worst sore throat ever, my eyes were burning, and when I got up, the world spun around for a minute before settling down. It was wonderful. I never felt so good in my life, despite feeling like hell, because I was still alive. And my horse was... he was *beautiful*. He'd filled out back to normal, drinking at least twenty gallons, maybe sucking even more out of the ground or wherever the pump was connected to, and his hair was *perfect*. I mean, he could have been coming from some horse beauty pageant or whatever like they used to have before the change.

But he was still a horse when he didn't need to be, and I was going to ask why when he whinnied and slobbered his tongue over my face. Then, his mouth right by my ear, he said quietly, "This place ain't right. I'm gonna stay a horse for a while. Just in case."

It only took five minutes to survey the buildings from the outside. It was an old-west town in miniature, with a saloon, a general store, a telegraph office (but no wires or poles), and a stage station with an attached stable that housed neither horses nor coaches. The rest of the buildings were either private homes or just didn't have signs outside saying what they were. Back east when I was a kid, I used to watch old movies on one of the last videoplasts that was still working at Chapel Hill, and this place had the look of the westerns they made before the change.

There wasn't a single person to be seen anywhere around. Looking through the glass window of the general store (the other establishments had wooden windows latched shut), I saw it was dark inside. The door was locked, so I went on to the saloon. That door opened when I pushed on it, but with the windows shuttered I couldn't see much to begin with.

"What the hell," I said, not specifically to my horse, who just happened to be standing nearby, and I walked inside.

The room was pretty dark, but apart from the light through the doorway which cut off as the door swung closed, some sunlight filtered through cracks in the shutters. It took a minute for my eyes to adjust, but then I could see well enough not to trip over anything. A bunch of wood tables were scattered around the room. Behind the brass-railed bar on the far wall, there were shelves of shot-glasses and steins, two big kegs and a double row of bottles. There was no debris, no sand, no dust even. Couldn't be more than a couple of days since it was cleaned. But the place was obviously empty, so I headed out again.

Back with my horse, I pretended to mess around with his cinch and so on, in case anyone was watching, and under my breath I muttered. "You're right. This place is impossible. If we hadn't just almost gotten killed getting here, if there wasn't a chance of finding something to help the folks back east, I'd want to turn around right now. You got any ideas?"

He shook his silver-maned head. "Nothing. What're you gonna—" He jerked a little and I saw the way he was looking. There was motion behind the windows of the general store.

"I'm checking it out," I said, and walked that way, my hand not far from my holster. My horse ambled along behind me, casual like he was just following me the way any old horse might do. I got close and saw a man in there, standing behind a counter. Well, what was I going to do? I opened the door and walked inside.

"Howdy, miss." The man was around fifty, salt and pepper hair with a walrus mustache. He was wearing an apron over a gray three-piece suit with a black ribbon tie. Except that he was dressed like an actor in one of those old movies, he seemed pretty normal to me. "What can I do you for?"

"I, uh...."

"New in town, miss? Just come in?"

"Yeah."

"Well, we got a little of everything in this shop. But if we don't got it, you ain't getting it, cause this's the only shop in town." He chuckled. "Now then, want some rolling tobacco? Some snuff? Trail rations? Ammo?"

I'd got some of my composure back by now.

"Some information would be nice," I said.

"I got some of that. And it's on sale, too: free today. What you want to know?"

"Okay. First off, where is everybody?"

The man frowned. "Not sure what you mean by that, missy. This ain't exactly a big town."

"I mean you're the only person I've seen so far."

"Oh, well.... No one in their right mind's going to walk around at noon in the high summer, are they? But you check out the saloon, I'm sure you'll find a passel of folk. And if you're new in town, I recommend it, cause you can probably get a room there for the night too."

I was going to complain that I just had, but I decided to leave it be.

"Second thing, I heard Pioche was bigger than this. Like ten times bigger."

"Pioche?" He laughed, cut himself off. "Not laughing at you, miss. But this here is Rachel. Population 34. Don't know about no Pioche, 'mafraid."

I traded him a .45 cartridge for a string of rock candy and got out of there without asking him about where he got all his stuff, or about the telegraph office with no wire and the stage station with no horses. The whole deal was too weird for me just then.

When I got back to him, my horse told me, "Just saw someone go into the saloon. And now there's music coming out of the place."

"Uh, huh." I told him what the shopkeeper had told me. That this was Rachel, not Pioche.

"Don't make much difference to me. Shouldn't be here, either way."

"I know."

"I'm scared," he said. "There's something bad here."

I'd never even imagined my horse might be scared of anything. I wanted to hug and comfort him, but I didn't because it would've looked weird if anyone was watching. So I just muttered in his ear, instead.

"I'm scared, too. But I guess we better check out that saloon again. Be silly to run away without finding anything out, right?"

"Suppose so," he said, but he didn't mean it.

Before I even got to the door, I could see the window shutters were open, and I could hear a piano playing inside. And when I entered, there wasn't just one person in the room but eight, the saloon keeper behind the bar, two cowboy-looking men bellied up to the bar with a bottle between them, four townies sitting around a table playing cards, and a piano-player at a small upright I hadn't noticed the first time through. He was smoking a cheroot and playing "Beautiful Dreamer." But where had they come from? My horse had only mentioned one person going in, and he could hardly have missed the others.

There's a standard scene in those old movies where the gunslinger steps into the saloon and the music stops and everyone stares at him. Not this time. Everyone just kept on doing what they were doing. None of them looked to be armed, and at first glance they seemed like ordinary folks except for the old-time outfits. I hesitated because right now more than anything I wanted to get on my horse and head on out of this place. But I steeled myself and walked up to the bar.

"Howdy," I said, because that's how it goes in the movies, and the saloon keeper nodded at me. She was a tall woman with weathered brown skin and rich russet hair, not young or old, and her eyes were an amazing apple green. But there was something cold about her appearance, something cruel hiding behind her smile. I realized I'd seen the same thing in the shopkeeper's face, but I'd shrugged it off. In the woman, it seemed more blatant, more forceful, and more terrifying too.

"What'll you have?" she asked.

"Whiskey," I managed, still pretending I was in a movie. "Straight up."

She slapped a shot-glass down on the bar top with a satisfying crack and filled it just to the rim from an unlabeled bottle.

I tapped it back. Not bad. At this point something was supposed to happen, like a bad guy barging in, but nothing did.

"You take barter?" I asked.

She shook her head. "We don't get many visitors. Your drinks're free. Welcome to Rachel."

She poured me another; I drank it in two sips. Warmth blossomed in my throat and belly. I could feel the buzz, which was alarming after just two shots, but I guess the almost-dying-of-thirst thing takes it out of you. No one paid me much attention; the saloon keeper didn't say anything more; and no gunmen showed up, either. I sighed. Wasn't going to get anywhere this way.

At last I said, "Little town like this, I figure if anyone's in charge, it's the saloon keeper."

She smiled, showing white, even teeth. "Mebbe so."

"Don't want to be rude," I said.

"You ain't been yet."

"Okay, then. What the actual fuck is going on here?"

I said that pretty loud, and this time I got a reaction from the room. The piano guy stopped playing; the four at the table turned to look at me; and the two men further down the bar turned, too. No one spoke at all for a moment.

"Fair question," said the saloon keeper, then, and the others turned back to their piano, their drinks, and their game. "I ain't gonna answer it today."

"But—"

"Gonna set you up with a boarding house room across the way, draw you a bath, get you some dinner later, let you have a night's rest on a proper bed, then tomorrow'll be for answers. 'Kay?"

I hesitated. All those things sounded pretty good, I had to admit. I was worn down with travel and dehydration, not to mention a whole lot of worrying. It wasn't like I could just make her talk if she didn't want to, anyway. "Okay."

"Good! Petey, show her a room, make sure it's set up nice, and Jen, you do her bath, you hear?"

Two of the card-players got up. They all looked different from one another, but I thought they had the same hard eyes, the same meanness lurking behind their bland expressions. The man tipped his hat, and the woman smiled at me. "I'll start the hot water," she said, and left ahead of me.

"Right this way," said the man, and I followed him outside.

"Got to see to my horse, first."

"Sure thing. Stable ain't seen much use lately, but there should be some oats and dried fruit and like that still there." He pointed across the way. "That place'll be yours tonight. I'll just make sure you got clean sheets and all, and when you're done with your horse, Jen'll have your bath ready for you too."

I led my horse over to the little stable, caught him up to date on what was going on.

"I don't know," he said. "It just ain't natural, none of this is."

I thumped his side. "You should talk, horse."

"You know what I mean."

"Yeah. I know. And I know you're natural, too; just a little weird, is all."

He licked my face and I had to laugh. "Want some rock candy?"

"That stuff'll rot your teeth," he said. "But I'll keep watch. Anything come up, just shout and I'll get you out of it."

"Will do."

The hot bath turned out to be the third nicest thing I'd ever had done for me. The second nicest was dinner: a delicious roast with greens and potatoes on the side plus a bowl of cold ice cream afterwards. The nicest came when the sun finally set, and I went to bed. Just as I'd settled in among the crisp white linens and the fluffy pillows and the soft down comforter, I heard a rapping at the shuttered window. I went to look with my gun in my hand, and there he was.

"Horse!"

"Sorry," he said, "I just couldn't bear it no more. You gonna let me in?"

"Get in, quick, before someone sees you!"

He clambered through the window in his human form, silver-blue skin and long shimmery-metallic hair and every other part of him exposed because he wasn't wearing any clothes.

I was going to play at being angry with him, but the truth is I couldn't wait any more myself, so I threw myself at him, and he caught me like I was nothing; and he carried me to that bed. You don't need to know any more than that what we did, except I'll say he didn't ever get tired, he could tell, somehow, every-thing I wanted and when I wanted it, and when what I wanted was to satisfy him, he let me do that too. In the end, I knew that I had done just that, satisfied him I mean, and I went to sleep in his arms.

When I got up the next morning, the new-risen sun pouring bloody light through my open window, I felt kind of tragic not having my horse there. Of course, he'd snuck out after I fell asleep to go back to being a horse again and not alarm the locals, assuming the locals were capable of being alarmed, which I wasn't so sure of.

I walked over to the stable first thing, and my horse was fine, but "Ghost town again," he said. "I'm pretty sure there was nobody in any of the houses overnight."

"Shit. You're the one who knows about magic. And you got no idea?"

"I didn't go to no school for this stuff," he said. "So I don't know what all is going on here. I'll tell you one thing, though, I did figure out."

"Yeah?"

"You know I can dowse pretty good. Well, when we first got

here, I was so thirsty I didn't stop to wonder where all this water they had was coming from."

"I don't blame you. I think I lost half an hour myself, just pumping and drinking."

"Ha," he said. "The two of us, snuffling around in that trough together. I bet we looked cute."

"You think they were watching?"

"Dunno. Probably maybe, I guess? But what I wanted to say is on the way back here last night, I stopped by the trough again, cause water's good, right? Except this time I tried to figure out where it was coming from. In my head, like. And I followed it a long way. There's some kind of cistern thing right there below the pump, but it's got a channel the water feeds into. And it ain't like regular groundwater, a layer down there mixed in with the earth. It's like a goddamn pipe is what it is. It goes down and down all the way."

"All the way?"

"All the way to the center."

"You don't mean the center of the Earth, do you, horse?"

He tossed his head. "Dunno. Know it's impossible, but that's what it seemed like to me. But that's not all. I was following that water channel and I felt it, something else down there. Something mixed in with the water"

"You don't know what it was?"

"Nope. Powerful stuff, though. Almost scary. I had the feeling I knew it from somewhere, too. But I couldn't remember where. Frustrating."

"Okaaay. Anything you think I should do about it?"

"Sorry," he said. "I really got no idea. Just thought you should know."

I left him then and ambled over to the saloon. The door was open, but with no one inside. There was a platter on one of the tables, though, with griddle cakes, eggs, bacon, hash-browns, and coffee, piping hot like it just came out of the kitchen, not that this saloon even had a kitchen. Like whoever made it knew I was going to be coming just this minute and started cooking it at the right moment fifteen minutes ago or whatever. And it occurred to me I hadn't wondered last night where my dinner came from, either. No animals here, no crops, and all this food looked and tasted fresh and delicious.

"Hope you liked it."

I'd just finished my last bite. I looked up and there she was, the saloon keeper behind the bar like she'd always been there.

"It was great," I said. "Haven't eaten this well since— all my life, I guess."

"Thanks. Always like to see a person who enjoys their food."

Her words were just what you'd want them to be if you were me, friendly and kind and all that. But there was that something in her face that scared me. I wished I didn't have to be there, that I didn't have to be beholden to her, but I couldn't think of any way out of this situation.

At last I said, "I guess you're not even pretending anymore you're regular folks."

"Never said we were, did we?"

She had me there. "But why all the play-acting and... why all this?"

"We going to get started on real talking, we better have your friend here too, don't you think?"

Figures she knew all along. I got hot for a minute, thinking maybe she was watching us last night, and then I shrugged inside. Not like it mattered, really.

"Okay," I said, "I'll get him."

"No need. I'll do it." But she didn't move, just smiled at me in a way she might have meant to be kindly, but I thought looked downright vicious. Like a cougar, maybe, or one of those griffins we were starting to get back east, contemplating a deer with a broken leg, anticipating a meal. A minute later the man she'd called Petey led my horse into the saloon. He was in his human form, dressed this time in clean new denim, cowboy boots, and a T-shirt that read "Welcome to the Little A'Le'Inn" and had a picture of a bug-eyed critter on it.

My horse took a chair at my table, scooted it over so I could feel his presence and put his hand on my shoulder. I felt nerves I didn't know were tensed up calming down, and I put my hand on his, and we just looked in each other's eyes for a bit. It was rude, maybe, but whatever. I glanced up and Petey was gone, vanished I guess back to wherever he'd come from, but the saloon keeper was still there, staring at us.

"I promised I'd give you answers," she said, "but first, tell me why you came. I mean, I know why, but it wasn't no easy journey, that's for sure."

"I guess that's fair," I said. "You know how fucked up things are back east?"

"Maybe I do," she said. "But tell me, anyway."

"Every year, the desert takes more land. Crops are failing, they never grew right after the change, but lately they're even worse. Seed's no good anymore. What wildlife is left is mostly mutants and monsters. The ocean's poisoned too, it's all salt and green slime, and there's no fish left. We're dying out, is what's happening."

"Bad news," she said. "But why come here?"

"We still got a few things left over from before the change. Videoplasts and some comps and phones and stuff that run on solar and don't need a network. Some folks who study the old times, they were looking into how the change started. And they found out two things. First, the change seems like it began here, a hundred years ago or so. Second, before the change there was a place around here called Area 51. Supposed to be a place where aliens came, space aliens, you know?"

"Like on this shirt your Petey gave me," offered my horse.

The saloon keeper said. "Yep. That's a gen-u-ine pre-change tourist-trade shirt you got there, boy."

I took a closer look at it. I wasn't impressed. Seemed kinda shoddy, really. But then it was over a hundred years old.

"Anyway," I said, "It wasn't much of a hope, but those... those scholars figured that there was nothing else they could do to fix things, and there was at least a chance something could be found out from around here. They asked me because with my horse we stood a chance of getting through the desert. And if there *were* such things as space aliens, they might be the only ones who could help us, if we could just convince them to do it."

"Seems mighty thin to me."

"Yeah. But we had nothing better to try. And as we traveled out west, we began to hear stories about a town still hanging on in the middle of nowhere. No one had been out that far west for years and years because of the desert, but there were still stories being told. Last settlement with people was Grand Junction, and they named the place. Pioche, they said it was. So we wanted to find out if the stories were true, and—"

"And you found us."

"Yeah. Is it my turn to ask questions yet?"

"Almost. What about you, Mr. Kayful Door? Why are you here?"

"That ain't my name," said my horse.

"No, but it's what you are. What the old-time Celts used to call your kind. Water-horse. And if you got a name, why don't your girl here use it?"

"She ain't my girl. I'm her horse."

"The hell I'm not," I said. And he looked at me and I looked at him, and we had another of those moments, but this time we were sharing something, something that said *don't trust her more than you can throw her.*

The saloon keeper walked out from behind her bar and sat

down at our table. I had to force myself not to shy away from her.

"Now it's my turn," she said. "Lemme give you some ancient history. Once upon a time history, right?"

"Okay, shoot."

"Once upon a time, there was something big and scary outside the world, and it wanted to eat all the world's magic."

"Wait up. There wasn't any magic before the change."

"But there was. Way far back. Anyhow, the world-spirit back then figured she couldn't fight the thing, the eater, so she hid all the magic away in a secret world down deep inside this one where the bad old thing couldn't find it. That was the first change, when all the magic in the world went away. And almost all the magic folk with it. Like you, Mr. Horse."

"Hold up," he said. "I never—"

"Yeah, you're special. Stubborn-like, I bet, so you didn't go with 'em, and you must've turned into a dumb old horse for a long time before the change woke you back up again. Wonder how you got here from Wales, anyhow. Must have been quite a story."

"Don't remember," he said. "Don't remember anything from back then. Only thing I remember now is Sooz finding me running wild a couple years back. She woke me right up."

The saloon-keeper shrugged. "Anyhow, the world-spirit's trick worked for a time. The eater went away and ate some other worlds instead. Just sucked 'em dry. But after a while it come back. Cause it was starving by then, starving to death almost. It had run out of food, and even with no magic around it still liked eating the life out of a world, 'cause that was better than nothing. So it latched onto this world, eating and eating, and after a while it found the secret world where the great spirit was hiding, and it drug her back out again. So we got the second change, the two worlds connected again, with magic coming back and all, but with the world pretty well ruined due to all the eating the big bad had already done."

"That sucks for us, then."

"Don't it? But anyways, there's always been a few connecting spots between the worlds, because they were never completely separate. And it turns out this place is one of them."

"What?"

"Yeah. The eater struck here first, 'cause it sensed a way down to the spirit world. That's why it's so dead everywhere around here 'cept this little spot, where there's a link all the way down there."

"You sure got a way of not answering a question and taking forever about it, too," said my horse.

The saloon keeper kept her face calm, but inside I felt like she was snarling. It took her a moment to answer, then she said, "You got me there. Been a long time since I had anyone to talk to but my own shadows. What did you want to know that I ain't telling?"

My horse said, "First off, what's the deal with this place? Why the fake town and fake people? And second, we need help, not stories. We're dying off. We don't care about the old world, where magic come from, nothing like that. We don't got the time to care."

"I was getting there. But to answer you straight, I've been stuck here for a hundred years all alone. Maybe I went a little crazy after a while. Got to distracting myself with games and such, but all this time I was sending out a calling, too. Hoping to snag some folks like you to brave the desert and make it here. Anyhow, it took me a while to wake up and get back to myself after you finally showed. Sorry 'bout that."

She smiled again, and it seemed to me like she was showing her fangs more than being polite, but she didn't seem to realize what it looked like, just kept on talking.

"So that was your number one. Number two, I got all this

reserve... essence you could call it, magical stuff, stored up from back when the two worlds were separate. Stored way down deep, along with all that other world's water. But I'm stuck here 'cause of this damn desert."

"That's a problem for you?"

"Yeah. See it's totally dead, so I can't cross it myself. I can only go where there's living stuff, at least a little of it. Been stuck here all this time, hoping someone like you would come. And here you are. So all you got to do is carry me across.... And I'll do it. I'll fix the world."

I guess she'd been building to this the whole time, but it still felt like she hit me between the eyes with a mallet. I had to ask. "You're her? The world-spirit you were talking about?"

"Used to be, anyways. Maybe will be again someday."

"Okay. Okay. What about the eater? Isn't it still waiting to get you?"

"Oh no," she said. "It's dead now. Or it's gone. Think it starved to death. So I can come out. That's why you're here, you understand? I called you. Your scholars back east, they heard me, and those refugees in Colorado, they heard me, and you heard me too, down deep somewhere, which is why you came all this way across the desert even though you nearly got your-selves killed doing it."

My horse took my hand, and he didn't say anything, but I could tell what he was thinking. Not because magic or what-ever but because, well, yeah. There was no way we were going to have any chance to talk this out without her listening in on us. I just had to hope she didn't know what I was thinking, and that she didn't know people enough to be able to guess, either. So I squeezed my horse's hand, and he smiled at the saloon keeper and said, "So, what do we gotta do, then?"

∾

THREE DAYS LATER, we were back in that damn desert again, this time heading straight home instead of wandering around like before. By my reckoning, we were about halfway between Rachel and the beginning of the regular kind of desert with scrub and scorpions and groundwater, where the saloon keeper said she wanted to get to. She'd jogged beside us for three days, totally unaffected by the heat, the lack of water, everything. She just kept a hand on my horse the whole time, even while we were sleeping, I guess because of that connection to something living she said she needed.

The sun was just setting, the red orb glowering on the western horizon like a bloodshot eye. My horse pulled up to a stop, and I dismounted. Around here, the desert was a flat salt plain, broken up into big cracked tiles like someone's messed up bathroom floor from before the change. There was a thin layer of fine sand on top of everything, but not so much you couldn't feel the hard desert floor under your feet. Hard enough so my horse clip-clopped on top of it, instead of punching through the crust with his hooves.

"Time to camp?" asked the saloon keeper.

"Nope," I said. "Time to say goodbye."

"Say what, now?"

I drew my revolver and pointed it at her, just in case it would do some good. You never know. "This is where you get off."

Give her credit. She didn't waste our time pretending she had no idea what I was talking about.

"How long did you know?"

"Almost from the start," I said. "I mean, you're creepy as hell. But when you said the eater had died just like that, I was certain."

"Damn. I went to a lot of trouble making that food for you, too. Didn't work, huh?"

"Yeah, no. Figures you'd put in extra effort on stuff to eat."

She shrugged. "So, what's your plan? Going to shoot me? Is that it?"

"Plan?" I shook my head. "No plan. Just figured you can't get across the desert without us, and it'd be best to ditch you right in the middle of it. And that part of what you told us must be true, too, or you'd already've eaten us all up, back east. Somehow you got trapped here, I guess. Maybe the real world-spirit sucked you in, if you didn't make her up. But either way, best if you just die right here, I mean, begging your pardon."

"You figuring to die along with me?"

My horse flinched at that, and I think he would have reared up and pulled back from her, but the saloon keeper was keeping some kind of grip on him, even though she just had a hand up on his withers, and he shuddered and rolled his eyes when he found he couldn't break away.

"We only got a few years left anyways," I said. "No sense in dragging it out. Best night I'm ever going to have I already had, thanks to you. It's all gonna be downhill from there. But we'll see what you can do in a minute. Maybe we won't die after all. Maybe you're just bluffing."

"The best night of your life, thanks to me. You don't feel bad about that? About stranding me here to die?"

"I sure do." I thumbed back the hammer on my gun. "Makes me sick to think about it. What you did for me. For us. Not so sick I'm not going to kill you, though."

The saloon keeper laughed. It was mean laughter, but it was honest, too. She really thought it was funny.

"All right," she said. "All right. You got me fair and square, but it don't matter. See, it was all over and done with when you got into Rachel and woke me up. Nothing you can do to me here. Guns sure won't work. I mean, you know what I am."

I looked into her eyes, and all at once I saw it. The spaces between the stars. The place she came from. The void. The darkness. The hunger. It was all there. I knew she was right. There wasn't any point in pulling the trigger.

"Okay," I said. "But you're still stuck here. If you could have crossed the desert on your own, you'd already have done it. We sure ain't taking you any further."

"Oh," she said. "You don't get it, do you? I don't need you, girl. I was just taking you with me for fun, so you could see what I was gonna do when I got free. What I need is *him*. And I got him, too."

My horse screamed then, and he did rear up, but she kept her grip on him. That's when I pulled the trigger. Six times, and I put six bullets in her, two in the chest, two in the head, right through her mean, snarling mouth, and two in the chest again. She staggered back, and blood gushed out of her, and for a moment I thought I might actually have done something. But then her body just fell apart into black smoky stuff, and it all swirled around my horse and into his nostrils and his eyes and like that, and he came down on his hooves all at once, like he wasn't comfortable with four feet anymore.

"Now, girl," he said, or she did, "you get up on my back, and I'll show you how the world ends."

A compulsion grabbed me, like I'd turned into a marionette. I dropped the gun I was trying to reload, and I stumbled over to my horse, herky-jerky. I found I could still talk, which was a relief. "What have you done to him?"

"Same thing I did to the world spirit. I'm inside your sweet little stallion, and he's inside me. And soon all of you little grub people will be in me, too. And every animal and every tree and every paramecium, but you'll be last of all. Ain't you lucky? And then I'll be moving on, and maybe I'll find somewhere new to eat, and maybe I won't, but you won't be around to care."

"You're inside him, too?" She was trying to make me mount up, but it was awkward, because she was having trouble getting my foot into the stirrup. It slipped out and I fell, and she made him laugh while she forced me back to my feet.

"That's right, girl. We're two parts of a whole, but I'm a million times stronger. That's how it goes. Everything I eat becomes me, sooner or later. He's fighting back, you know, but there ain't nothing he can do because I've eaten a million worlds and even diminished as I am, he's just one little old water-horse. Takes a while to digest folks, till they're all gone, you know. He'll be screaming on the inside, and you'll be screaming on the outside. Until the end of the world, and I eat you too. Ain't that nice?"

She got my foot seated in the stirrup this time, and she started puppeting me into the saddle.

"Well, okay then," I said. "In that case, Milafon Ysbrid, I name your true name, and I bind you to me."

"What?"

My horse reared up, and since I wasn't seated properly yet I just fell backwards off his rump. I landed hard, smacking my head against the salt tile floor, but nothing was broken. I could still talk, so I said, "Milafon Ysbrid, I name you. You are mine, and you always will be mine."

She screamed a terrible equine scream with his lungs, and I think she was trying to do something, to control me, to shut me up, maybe, but whatever magic or power she'd been using on me didn't work anymore, because it couldn't. I struggled to my feet. Too late it occurred to her, she was in a horse's body, and she could maybe stomp me with it, but even as she was turning to try it, I told her, "Milafon Ysbrid! I've named you three times! You're mine, now and forever!"

And it was true. I could feel him now, and her too, like they were both part of me. It was like I'd grown a second heart, a huge and powerful one too, only it was rotten with cancer, shot through with corruption, and in its center, a kernel, a seed, a mote of infinite coldness and darkness— An awful thing, the eater of worlds, but she was mine now, just like he was, and there was nothing she could do to resist my will.

I took a step toward my horse, and I put my hand on his soft nose. He made a terrible choking noise, and he snorted out a writhing wormy thing, cold from the depths of interstellar space, right into my hand. I dropped her to the ground, and ground my boot heel into her, and because she was part of me, I could feel her breaking up, dissipating, and fading away. It was like having my heart cut out of me then, and I staggered and would have fallen except my horse had his arms around me and was holding me up.

"Told you I wanted you to bind me," he whispered into my ear.

"Oh yeah? What's my name, then?"

"Susannah, but— oh, you don't mean it, do you?"

"I do," I said. "My full name. Three times."

"It ain't gonna work," he said. "It can't work. You're a human. You're not the kind to be bound. And even if it could, I couldn't be the one to bind you. It don't work that way."

"Try it."

"But—"

"For me," I said. "Please. It's what I want."

He stopped protesting. "Susannah Leah Apterbach, will you be mine?"

"Forever," I said.

He told me my name twice more; and I could feel the balance shifting, and like that I was a part of him, the same way he was a part of me. For a while we just sat there together holding hands, he in his human form, me in mine, exploring one another from the inside out, and by the time we were done, it was full dark and the stars were out, shining bright in the sky overhead.

"Well, okay, then," he said at last. "So it did work. But about that forever thing, the world you know, we only got—"

"A few more years? I think we got more than that, horse."

"What?"

I pointed. "Three days, thataway. All the water the world-spirit got stowed away in her secret world. All the essence stuff the eater latched onto to make that faked-up town. It's all there, and it's waiting for us."

"But—"

"You'll see. It's all going to work out. We're two parts of a whole, now, can't you feel it? It's all there waiting for us."

"Oh... oh, yeah. It really is."

"Come on then," I told him. And a minute later, if you'd been there, you'd've seen two horses, a stallion and a mare, galloping side by side through the desert, galloping together under the bright shining stars.

FUR AND FEATHER

INGRID L. TAYLOR

T he meadow had been hers for as long as it had taken the flowers to pass through one cycle of blooming and fading. She had defended against the larger birds, the crows and the sparrows, as yellow sun had given way to the pale autumn. The memory of her mother's nest had dimmed, and she learned to treasure the solitary rustle of the grasses and the slow darkening of days. The coyote came with the smell of rain. She heard him at night as he passed around the edge of her meadow, keeping to the shelter of the trees.

Though it was not in the hummingbird's nature to seek companionship, she felt a fascination for the coyote that slowly grew into love as the sleeting winter rains faded into the warm drizzle of spring. She loved him for his lonely howl that rang clear and mournful on the cold nights when she was tucked away in her nest, and she thought that someone who made a sound so beautiful surely couldn't be bad. She was a creature of the daytime, of sunlight and flowers and sweet nectar. She was flighty as well, dashing from one flower to the next, never wanting to give a single bloom too much of her attention. She sensed a depth and steadiness in the coyote where she might rest her pounding wings and calm her racing heart.

The coyote came to the beach at the edge of the woods in the early mornings. He ate the crabs that washed up on the shore, and she watched him savor the salty crunch of their shells. Sometimes he ate the seaweed too, when hunting was lean. She imagined the cool sand was soft on the pads of his feet, and the brine soothed his throat, hoarse from his nightly offerings to the moon.

She found excuses to leave her meadow and come down to the beach, hovering over the white flowers of blackberry bushes that tangled the border from forest to shore and taking in their sparse nourishment. The coyote lay down in the sand with a crab shell propped between his paws. His canines gleamed in the early light of morning. The surf sang its endless song. It was the hour of possibility, when the moon and sun touched fingertips before they went their separate ways, and their children, the stars, closed their luminous eyes.

The hummingbird flew to the coyote and hovered above his muzzle, which was flecked with shell fragments and sea salt. His ears pricked forward, and he lifted a paw to swat at her. She

avoided it easily—she was fast. The coyote stretched his lips
back, and his tongue lolled from the side of his mouth.

"Who are you?" he asked.

She did not often speak to the four-legged animals, only the
birds that shared the air with her, and once, a wayward cat that
had passed through her meadow. She had fluffed out all of her
feathers and buzzed the cat's head, shrieking at him to leave
her territory. Now unsure what to say to the coyote, she took off
down the beach, zigging and zagging. He chased her, his body
stretched to full length as his feet pounded the sand.

She paused above a fallen log, and he sat and panted at her
with his pink tongue. The sunlight slanted off her, and the wet
sand steamed as the sun rose in the sky. Soon it would be time
for him to go.

The coyote rested his chin on the log, his eyes a soft brown
like chestnuts that fell to the forest floor. She perched on the
log and folded her wings, certain now he wouldn't hurt her. He
blew his hot breath on her. Her feathers lifted with the force of
it, and she was changed in that moment—no longer a creature
of air and light but weighted by the burden of meat and bone
and soil that invited the decaying flesh.

The heat of the new day pressed upon her, and the coyote
was gone. She caught a last glimpse of his bushy tail as he
disappeared into the forest.

Day after day, the hummingbird and coyote played together
on the beach. Sometimes the chase was long and sometimes it
lasted for only a few minutes. At those times, they rested
together on the log. She gripped his wiry fur in her tiny feet
and curled up on his back, and worried about the outline of his
ribs that showed beneath his coat. His food was taken by creatures who left shiny metal teeth on the forest floor, mouths that
didn't devour but maimed and imprisoned. She had heard the
cries of the animals caught. The creatures brought the scent of

panic and fear, so strong that even she could smell it. It permeated the forest, and darkness spread. Flowers bloomed less brightly, their nectar was less sweet, and she had to fly farther every day to find fuel for her demanding body.

One morning the coyote didn't come to the beach. She waited on the log, wings folded, until the sun was high overhead and the aroma of rotting kelp and dead fish choked the air. The surf rushed in and covered the sand. Pebbles, caught helpless in the unyielding grip of the waves, tumbled and rolled. The hummingbird watched them as the air closed around her. She looked behind her to the woods. She knew its meadows and clearings, but she had never ventured into the entangled mass of trees and underbrush that made up its dense center. Her heart fluttered, and she was afraid.

Dewdrops clung to blades of grass in defiance of the rising heat of the day. The meadow sparkled in the morning light. Petals swayed in choruses of white, purple, and yellow. She dipped her tongue into a bloom and lapped up the nectar. Its energy flowed through her, and her wings pumped harder and faster. She ascended, higher and higher, until the individual flowers coalesced into a rainbow of color below her. She flew into the woods.

She had always imagined dark and impenetrable undergrowth, but beneath the redwood canopy she saw a loamy path dappled with sunlight and dotted with small bushes. The air was wet. Pale mushrooms sprouted around the trunks of the trees, which were covered on one side with a carpet of green moss. She hovered, weighted by the ancient feel of the forest, and for the first time in her life the hummingbird sensed the depth of time, that all things pass into darkness.

"What are you doing here, little bird?" The owl sat nearby on a thick branch. His eyes gleamed in the dim light.

The hummingbird dashed behind a broad leaf.

"I'm looking for the coyote." Her voice was thin and high in the stillness between the trees.

The owl's eyes followed her, immense and yellow. "You would make a tasty snack before my bedtime, little hummingbird."

"Please— Will you help me find him?"

"Come out from behind that leaf, and I'll consider it."

The hummingbird moved from the leaf's camouflage, forcing herself to hover in front of the owl while her instincts screamed at her to flee.

"Have you seen him?"

The owl looked long and hard at her, then with a shake that ruffled all of his feathers, he settled deeper onto the branch. "You're lucky that I had a good night hunting. I won't eat you today. But your coyote was not so lucky. You'll find him ahead. Look for the biggest tree in the woods." The owl closed his eyes.

The hummingbird waited a moment, but the owl appeared to be asleep. As she zoomed past him, the owl muttered, "Evil roots in our home. Take care, little one."

She found the coyote beneath an ancient redwood. He lay on his side, his ribs heaving with each rasping breath. The metal teeth, no longer shiny but stained dark with his blood, gripped his front leg. He lay in a pool of mud and hair and torn skin. There were grooves in the dirt around him where he had dug in his claws, trying to escape.

"My love," she hovered over him, "how can I free you?"

He had bitten his tongue in his pain and frenzy, and his words were thick with blood. "I must chew my leg free, but I am too weak."

The hummingbird brought him drops of water from a nearby stream, held carefully in a leaf that she tipped into his mouth. She found some berries nearby and carried them, one by one to his lips, until she dropped exhausted onto a low bush.

"It is not enough." The coyote's voice was thin and strained. "Go quickly and find the beaver. She is strong enough to chew me free."

The hummingbird floated over him. "I don't want to leave you."

"Hurry— before these monsters come for me."

She flew as fast as she could to the beaver's den, though she was heavy with the scent of his blood and rent flesh.

The beaver poked her nose out. "What is all this shrieking and fluttering?"

"The coyote is trapped, and he can't free his leg. Come and chew him free with your powerful teeth."

"Why would I do that? He might devour me once he's free."

"Please, we don't have much time. He'll die if you don't help."

The beaver squatted on her round haunches. "Besides, I don't eat meat. I can't imagine the taste of it in my teeth. It's horrifying."

"You can spit it out. Please... I love him, and I don't want him to die."

The hummingbird's feathers drooped as the beaver gazed off into the distance. A breeze passed through, carrying the smell of dead fish and rotted wood. She thought of their walks on the beach, and her heart crashed against her ribcage as if it would burst from the confines of her chest.

"All right. I'll do it, but he has to promise that he won't eat me."

The beaver's steady plod through the forest was agonizing for the hummingbird. The sun slanted low in the sky when they reached the place where the coyote was trapped.

He was gone. Only a scattered pile of bloody leaves remained. A strange sensation permeated the air, sharp and violent, like nothing the hummingbird had encountered before.

She flew in furious circles over the area, looking for any sign of him. There was only the silence of the darkening forest. The beaver hung her head, and after a moment she ambled back in the direction of her den. The hummingbird watched her go and knew no word or gesture could contain this moment. There was only the bright pain that washed through her.

In the following days, the pain transformed to a sorrow that muted the shine of her feathers to a dull gray. She sat in a bush by the meadow and watched flowers nod in the wind. She thought often of the beach but couldn't bear to return.

One early morning she could no longer stand the rustle of the meadow grass and the cloying cheerfulness of the flowers. She went to the beach, to the log where they had always met. The feel of the smooth driftwood under her feet caused fresh pain. She watched the waves topple pebbles and small sticks and thought that she could fly into those waves and disappear.

The bushes behind her rustled, and soft feet padded toward her. A four-legged creature stood on the beach looking at her. The creature had no fur, rather exposed muscle gleamed in the early light, outlined by veins and connective tissue. She drew back, frightened. It took a step towards her. She recognized the eyes of the coyote, though the long lashes and warm brown irises looked out of place in the wet redness of his face.

"I've waited for you," he said.

"You were gone when I came back. I looked and looked, but I couldn't find you."

"They have taken my skin and fur."

A fly buzzed around the face of the coyote, then passed through his head and continued down the beach.

The hummingbird fled, beating her wings as fast as she could to escape the horrible raw thing that her coyote had become. She stopped and hovered just at the edge of the beach, where the sand mingled with coarse grass. She could return to the meadow, live out her days among the flowers and grasses, and try to forget the vision of bare muscle and blood. But the coyote's eyes appeared before her, sad and lost. She remembered how much joy he had brought her, and she knew she couldn't leave him to his loneliness and pain.

She turned and raced back down the beach, where the coyote waited for her.

ABOUT THE AUTHORS

A. Katherine Black is an audiologist and a writer. She adores multicolored pens, stories featuring giant spiders, and almost everything at 2am. She lives in a house surrounded by very tall and occasionally judgmental trees, along with her family, their cats, and her overused coffee machines. Find her on flywithpigs.com or on twitter at @akatherineblack.

Laurence Raphael Brothers is a writer and a technologist with five patents and a background in AI and Internet R&D. He has published over 50 short stories in such magazines as *Nature*, *PodCastle*, and of course *Zooscape*. His noir urban fantasy books *The Demons of Wall Street*, *The Demons of the Square Mile*, and *The Demons of Chiyoda* are available from Mirror World Publishing, while his new standalone novel *The World's Shattered Shell* has just been published by Water Dragon. Pronouns: he/him. Website: https://laurencebrothers.com/

Luna Corbden (who also writes as Luna Lindsey) lives in Washington State. They are autistic and genderfluid. Their first story, about a hippopotamus, crawled out of their head at age 4.

After running out of things to say about hippopotami, they switched to sci-fi, fantasy, and horror. Their stories have appeared in the *Journal of Unlikely Entomology, Penumbra eMag,* and *Crossed Genres.* They tweet like a bird @corbden. Their novel, *Emerald City Dreamer,* is about faeries in Seattle and the women who hunt them.

Dylan Craine is an aspiring wizard who lives in someone's attic in Colorado with his three pets, all imaginary. He enjoys traveling beyond the limits of human ken, trading riddles with dragons, and reading. Every once in a galactic year, he can be spotted posting to his Twitter @dpwatrcreations or to his blog at . His other work has appeared in *Worlds Without Master.*

Matt Dovey is very tall, very English, and most likely drinking a cup of tea right now. He has a scar on his arm where his parents carved a rune into his humerus: apparently it was BISCUIT, and yes he would like another digestive, thank you for asking. He now lives in a quiet market town in rural England with his wife and three children, and still struggles to express his delight in this wonderful arrangement.

His surname rhymes with "Dopey" but any other similarities to the dwarf are purely coincidental. He has fiction out and forthcoming all over the place; you can keep up with it at mattdovey.com, or find him time-wasting on Twitter as @mattdoveywriter.

Voss Foster lives in the middle of the Eastern Washington desert, where he writes science fiction and fantasy from inside a single-wide trailer. He is the author of *Evenstad Media Presents* as well as the *Office of Preternatural Affairs.* His short work can be found across the internet, including *Alternative Truths, Vox.com,* and Flame Tree Publishing's *Heroic Fantasy.* His work often focuses on issues of diversity and inclusion, and always with a lyrical bent. When not writing, he can be found cooking, singing, cuddling the dogs, and of course, reading, though rarely all at the same time. More information can be found at http://vossfoster.blogspot.com.

Adele Gardner (they/them, Mx., gardnercastle.com) is a full/active member of SFWA and HWA with a poetry collection, *Halloween Hearts*, available from Jackanapes Press and fiction and poetry in *Analog, Clarkesworld, Strange Horizons, PodCastle, Flash Fiction Online,* and more. With eleven poems winning or placing in the Poetry Society of Virginia Awards, Balticon Poetry Contest, and Rhysling Award, Gardner serves as literary executor for father, mentor, and namesake Delbert R. Gardner.

Gwynne Garfinkle lives in Los Angeles. Her collection of short fiction and poetry, *People Change*, was published in 2018 by Aqueduct Press. Her work has appeared in such publications as *Strange Horizons, Uncanny, Apex, Through the Gate, Dreams & Nightmares, Not One of Us,* and *The Cascadia Subduction Zone.*

Diana A. Hart lives in Washington State, speaks fluent dog, and escapes whenever somebody leaves the gate open—if lost, she can be found rolling dice at her friendly local game store. Her passion for storytelling stems from a well-used library card and years immersed in the oral traditions of the Navajo. She was previously published in *Writers of the Future, Vol. 34.*
    Follow her on Twitter: @DianaAHart

Lucia Iglesias holds a B.A. from Brown University and is pursuing her MFA in Fiction at the University of Kansas. Home is Oakland or Iceland, depending on the time of year, and she is a friend of cats everywhere. Her work has appeared in *The Rumpus, Shimmer, Liquid Imagination, Cosmic*

Roots and Eldritch Shores, The Bronzeville Bee, and other publications.

Stella B. James is a Southern girl who appreciates strong coffee and losing herself in fantastical daydreams. When she isn't writing, she can be found reading romance novels of any genre, drinking Prosecco while watching whatever she has left over on her DVR, or talking herself out of buying yet another black dress. She has published several short stories with various publications that you can find on her website, www.stellabjames.com. Check out her Instagram @stellabjames, where she shares her writing and inner musings.

K.C. Mead-Brewer lives in Ithaca, NY. Her fiction appears in *Electric Literature's Recommended Reading, Joyland Magazine, Strange Horizons,* and elsewhere. She is a graduate of Tin House's 2018 Winter Workshop for Short Fiction and of the 2018 Clarion Science Fiction & Fantasy Writers' Workshop. For more information, visit kcmeadbrewer.com and follow her @meadwriter.

A Cincinnati resident, **Mark Mills** teaches composition, literature, philosophy, and film studies at Indiana Tech University and Chatfield College. He has published work in *Tor.com, Grievous Angel, Short Story America,* and several other publications. He has worked on and appeared in several low budget movies, including *Satanic Yuppies, Live Nude Shakespeare, Chickboxin' Underground, Zombie Cult Massacre,* and *Uberzombiefrau.* He currently is occupied with his family, a large number of animals, and many unpublished stories.

Lena Ng lives in Toronto, Canada, and is an active member of the Horror Writers Association. Her short stories have appeared in publications such as *Amazing Stories* and *Flame*

Tree's Asian Ghost Stories and *Weird Horror Stories*. Her stories have been performed for podcasts such as *Gallery of Curiosities, Creepy Pod, Utopia Science Fiction, Love Letters to Poe,* and *Horrifying Tales of Wonder. Under an Autumn Moon* is her short story collection.

Sandy Parsons is a Pushcart-nominated author and the winner of the 2022 ServiceScape fiction contest. Her fiction can be found in *Analog Science Fiction and Fact, Escape Pod,* and *Reckoning,* and others. In addition to writing fiction, Sandy narrates audio fiction. More information can be found at http://www.sandyparsons.com

Michael H. Payne's stories have appeared in places like *Asimov's Science Fiction,* a half dozen collections from FurPlanet, and 11 of the last 12 annual *Sword & Sorceress* anthologies, a run that includes the Ursa Major Award winning short story "Familiars." His novels have been published by Tor Books and Sofawolf Press, he's only posting 4 pages of webcomics a week these days instead of the 11 pages he did for over 15 years, and his poems turn up pretty regularly on the *Silver Blade* website and in the Rhysling Award anthologies. Check hyniof.com for further particulars.

David Steffen is the editor of *Diabolical Plots* and the cofounder and administrator of *The Submission Grinder.* His work has been published in very nice places like *Escape Pod, Intergalactic Medicine Show,* and *Podcastle,* among others. The rumors that he is the pupal stage of some kind of dog-cloud hybrid are exaggerations at best.

Ingrid L. Taylor is a writer, poet, and veterinarian. She lives in the desert with a houseful of cats, two large dogs, and a yard full of pigeons and hummingbirds. When she's not writing sad and creepy stories, she works as an editorial director for a veterinary publishing department. Her writing has most recently appeared in *Poet Lore, Artemis Journal, Black Fox Literary Magazine, Southwest Review, Collateral Journal,* and others. She has received support for her writing from the Pentaculum Artist Residency, Playa Artist Residency, Right to Write fellowship, Horror Writers Association, and Gemini Ink. For pictures of her animal family and updates on her writing, visit her at ingridltaylor.com and on Instagram @tildybear.

ABOUT THE EDITOR

Mary E. Lowd is a prolific science-fiction and furry writer in Oregon. She's had more than 200 short stories and a dozen novels published, always with more on the way. She has been nominated for the Ursa Major Awards more than any other individual, and her work has won three Ursa Major Awards, eleven Leo Literary Awards, and four Cóyotl Awards.

Mary was the co-chair of the Wordos critique group for five years and the chair of the Cóyotl Awards for eight years. She edited five volumes of FurPlanet's *ROAR* anthology series, and she is the editor and founder of the furry e-zine *Zooscape*.

She lives in a crashed spaceship, disguised as a house and hidden behind a rose garden, with an extensive menagerie of animals, some real and some imaginary.

Printed in the USA
CPSIA information can be obtained
at www.ICGtesting.com
JSHW020501070823
46061JS00001B/39

9 781088 214541